Beating a Dead Stick

Beating a Dead Stick

Herbert Knapp

Girandole Books, New York, NY

Publisher's Cataloging-in-Publication data

Names: Knapp, Herbert, 1931-, author.
Title: Beating a dead stick / Herbert Knapp.
Description: New York, NY: Girandole Books, 2016.
Identifiers: ISBN 978-0-9971646-3-3 | LCCN 2016916516
Subjects: LCSH Urban youth--Fiction. | High schools--Fiction. | High school students—Fiction. | Teachers--Fiction. | Murder--Fiction. | Mystery and detective stories. | BISAC FICTION / Mystery & Detective / General.
Classification: LCC PS3611.N355 B43 2016 | DDC 813.6--dc23

Text is in Minion Pro
Stylized text is in Dillon
Book designed by Steven M. Alper

Printed in the United States of America
First Girandole edition 2016

If the parents of each generation always or often knew what really goes on at their son's school, the history of education would be very different.

C.S. Lewis, *Surprised by Joy*

An Explanation

Gus (Augusta) found my manuscript in her father's desk after he died. (She's his daughter, not mine. I was his second wife.) "Is it true?" she asked. "Mostly," I said. "But who remembers every word of every conversation or what they were thinking at certain times and places? I made that stuff up."

She wanted to publish it. I told her nobody would be interested, it happened so long ago. She laughed and instantly googled up three news stories for me.

In 2012 in Lebanon, Ohio, a high school student was convicted of selling up to $20,000 worth of high-grade marijuana a month. He was a drug kingpin. He had six teenage lieutenants.

In 2014 in Sarasota, a high school student recruited her schoolmates for a prostitution ring and coordinated the trysts on Facebook, charging $50 to $100 in cash and alcohol.

And in 2015 in Spokane, Washington, the police arrested two teenage brothers, 15 and 17, who were promoting the prostitution of underage girls. The girls who didn't perform were ripped off or assaulted. The investigation got its start after the older brother was arrested in relation to a drive-by shooting. The police listened in on the calls he made from behind bars, hoping that would lead to more evidence about the shooting. Instead, they heard him instructing his brother on how to run the prostitution ring while he was in juvenile hall.

"It's still happening. Probably it's worse."

So I told her to do whatever she wanted with my memoir or confession—whatever it is. Her father was dead, and even if someone remembers the old scandal, it won't matter.

Major Characters in the order of their appearance, Chapters 1–9

Chapter 1

C all me crazy. You won't be the first. Last October—
October 18, 1987 (the day the stock market fell over
500 points) my car caught fire.

I hardly knew Didimo at the time. But yesterday—June,
21, 1988—his car crashed and burned right down at the corner
of my block. So what's the connection? "Shit happens," says
Vern. I can't accept that. Things do not just happen!

I am a painter. I've never sold anything. Never tried. I
paint pictures like Emily Dickinson wrote poems, up in my
room all by myself. I used to teach high school to pay for my
paint, canvases, and groceries. Ten days ago, I retired. I won't
be collecting social security for another twenty-three years,
but after my father died, we—my brother and I—inherited
some real estate. That's how come I can afford to retire.

I'm off the track. Okay, I was driving to work. It was dark
and raining. I was leaning forward, squinting at . . . is it "tail
lights" or "taillights"? Or is it hyphenated? Who cares, right?
I'm just not quite used to not being an English teacher anymore.

Okay, I was squinting at the tail lights ahead of me. I
braked when they came on and sped up when they went off.
A voice on my radio was urging me to buy something. Then

I smelled it. Then I saw it. Smoke was slithering out from under my dashboard. I—my car, that is—was on fire. DO SOMETHING! I shouted silently.

So I turned off the ignition. Well, that was "something," wasn't it? It seemed prudent. But then I saw a gas station on the other side of the highway and turned, intending to zoom across in front of the oncoming traffic. But, of course, when I pressed on the gas, nothing happened. Terrified, I coasted across three lanes of highway. Horns honked. Cars swerved and skidded. But I made it. I rolled into the service area, steered around the cars that were blocking my way— police cars, I realized later—broke through the yellow tape, and stopped under the high roof that came out over the pumps. Pushing open the door, I lurched out, almost falling and was caught by a man wearing a yellow slicker.

"Are you crazy, lady?"

Was I? My heart was beating so fast I couldn't speak.

Another yellow slicker said, "Lady, are you blind?"

That reminded me. "FIRE!" I yelled, pointing at the smoke inside my car.

They looked. Then one of them grabbed my left elbow; the other, my right. They hoisted me so I was kind of tippy-toeing as they rushed me into the gas station's office, where they parked me by the snack dispenser. From there I watched through the big window as two men wearing white coveralls ran from the garage bays with fire extinguishers. They raised the hood of my car and sprayed the engine.

"Do you have some identification, ma'am?"

I turned around. He was shorter than I am and younger— but not young. His collar was unbuttoned. There were grease spots on his tie, dark circles under his eyes, and he was gobbling fragments of potato chips from a bag that looked like he'd found it wadded up in his pocket.

"Hey," he said. "Miss Butler, right? I was in your third period. Hey, us guys thought you were hot stuff. I mean...I mean, you still are...I mean...Oh, shit." He grinned and blushed. "Still teachin'? How's it goin'? Kids giving you any trouble?"

"No more than usual."

"Take this. You notice anything at school, you give me a ring."

I took his card: "Detective Mark Miles." And then I placed him. Fourth row, halfway back. "Notice anything like what?"

"Oh, y'know. Unusual."

I kept looking at him, bemused by little Marky Miles who had grown up to be a real detective and who would— if he were cleaned up— be handsome enough to play a detective on some television show.

"You can go now."

I pulled myself together, and then I realized I couldn't go anywhere. "My car ..." I blurted.

He realized my problem and said something to a uniform who went to the door to the garage and said something to someone I couldn't see. I wanted to ask Mark what was going on. Why was he here? What had happened? But then in from the garage came a big, lanky kid in white coveralls who was rubbing his wet hair with a dirty towel. He took one look at me, stopped, and announced to the others, "Hey, this 's my old English teacher." Then, to me, he said, "You remember me, dont'cha?"

I stepped closer to check his name tag.

"Of course, Blaine."

He boosted me into the cab of the tow truck, and as he drove me to school I asked, "What happened back there? Was the station robbed?"

"Yeah. Robbed. And Ol' Bill—they shot him. Me 'n the boss—as soon as we got there, we sensed it. Yeah, before we even saw him. I keep seeing him there on the floor. Coulda been me, y'know. I work that shift sometimes. Oh, shit, shit, shit. Jeeze! Well, how's it goin' at my old alma mater? I bet you never had a class like ours, huh?"

"That's terrible. Was he ...?"

"Well, they took him to the hospital. I hope he makes it. Jeeze, there was blood everywhere. Hey, I bet you remember me as pretty much a troublemaker, huh? Yeah, but you know what? I got Saved."

"Saved," I repeated, staring at the rain and thinking of Old Bill, who had gone to work last night with no idea of what was going to happen. And here I was going to work this morning. with no idea about...

"In Revelations. You ever read it? Well, see, it says how just before the end, the air's gonna darken and the waters get polluted. So, hey, air pollution and the environment. Chemicals and stuff. You hear about that? Like it says, the heavens— they're gonna meet with fervent heat. And 'The earth also and all the elements therein.' But first we're gonna freeze. Like global cooling, Oh, and Babylon. The Middle East. That's where it's gonna start."

"Do you have a specific date in mind?"

"Oh, no ma'am. Like it says, 'The day and the hour knoweth no man.' But that don't make me no mind because whenever it comes, I'll be Raptured. You know about that? Being Raptured? Have you been Saved, Miss Butler?"

"Uh, well, I..."

"I got this problem, though. I'm in love."

"What's the problem?"

"Well, she's Catholic, and I'm not sure I can marry somebody who's not a Christian. Are you a Christian, ma'am?"

I sat up straighter, ready to say something sarcastic but realized he wouldn't "get it." Nobody "got" anything anymore. And anyhow, what good did it do to be snotty?

"Here y'are. Pershing High—the old alma mater."

Turning up my collar, I started to get out, but didn't. I was thinking. about Ol' Bill.

"'Samatter? Y'worried 'bout cher car? No prob. Hey, couple days. You give us a ring. We can't close. The boss—he's got bills to pay. Us guys, we got bills to pay. We don't get no timeout on accounta ol' Bill."

"Thanks for the ride, Blaine."

I pushed the door shut, but not before I heard him call, "God bless."

Chapter 2

"Hi," said a perky young woman.

She came closer—too close—using her umbrella to shield us both from the rain—except that it had stopped raining. "Do we know each other?" I asked, trying to sound perky, too.

"Are you a teacher? Because me, too—going to be. I start my practice teaching today. I'm Pris."

Mystery solved. "Glad to meet you, Pris. I believe Stella Yavorov's going to supervise you."

"Yeah, that's what they said at first, but now they say I'm with a guy named Butler."

"Butler? I'm Barbara Butler."

"Wow! How come I thought you were a guy? I guess I figured all Butlers were guys, huh?"

We walked towards the school. It was built in 1924 and looks like a cross between a factory and a castle. Students were getting off buses and waiting for the doors to open. A girl ran up to me waving an envelope.

"Here. For college. You need to write about me."

"This doesn't have a stamp on it, Cady."

"Come on, Cady!" bellowed a distant friend.

"Hey, it's official or somethin' 'n't it?" She flashed me an enormous smile and dashed off. "Gotta go," she called back.

I looked around for my new friend. She had gone on ahead and was up near the top of the front steps where a boy wearing a ski mask was blocking her way. He exhaled a plume of smoke into her face. The kids around them laughed.

I couldn't get through the crowd. No one moved aside for me. Then I saw Didimo. He was watching me. Whenever his name came up in the faculty lounge, someone would say, "That kid is bad news." But he was in my study hall last year, and he never gave me any trouble. We made eye contact. That was all. But then he turned and called out, "Ray!"

The boy in the ski mask stepped aside, and the crowd loosened up.

"Teachers go in the side door," I explained, leading Pris away. "This entrance is just for students."

"But isn't that discrimination?"

A janitor let us in the side door, but we were only halfway down the dim, echoing hallway when the first bell buzzed. I grabbed my new friend's arm and forced her to trot. Students were surging into the building behind us, filling the hall with loud conversations, hoots and shrieks.

"Hasn't anyone ever complained?" Priscilla demanded, trying to pull away from me. "About the discrimination?"

Almost running, we rounded the corner, and I pulled open the door to the main office. But my principal, one arm raised to push open the door I was pulling open from the other side, came staggering forward out into the hall and collided with Pris. They embraced and did a little waltz turn as students flowed around us.

"Dr. Windmuller," I shouted, "this is Priscilla, uh..."

"Wentworth," she shouted.

"Wentworth," I shouted. "Practice teacher. Pris, this is our principal, Dr. Windmuller."

They stopped dancing. Arnold stepped back, panting, and tapped his chest. "Arnold," he said. "No honorifics around here. Need to talk. Feel free. Communication. Key to excellence. Have a good day."

I blocked his escape. "I need to talk to you," I said. "Miss Wentworth thinks I am supposed to supervise her."

"No! Not now, not now."

Shouldering me aside, he slipped into his private office across the hall.

I looked around for Priscilla. Gone again. So I went into the main office. At the front counter, a boy was talking to his friends while a streak of blood slid down the side of his face. A girl kept reporting to no one in particular that a toilet on the third floor was overflowing. Phones were ringing. Teachers and student assistants were hurrying back and forth. A voice coming from the loudspeaker set high in the wall said Number 36 had broken down and would be late.

Shirley Zahn (the school secretary) was talking alternately into two phones, trying to find substitutes for the teachers who had called in sick. Max Tinder (social studies) was standing in front of her complaining that there was no paper for the copy machine. She gazed at him blankly, which caused him to wave his arms and talk louder. Then I saw the Wentworth girl. She had found the watering can that Shirley kept behind the filing cabinets and was watering the violets on the windowsill.

I took a deep breath and went over to the teachers' mail boxes where I took the day's memos and announcements from my box. Stepping back to sort them, I bumped into Bert Kumpf (math), who was dropping the memos and announcements he'd just taken from his mailbox into the giant wastebasket that was kept there to receive them.

"Everything..." he began.

We finished together: "...is fundamentally simple."

It's Bert's mantra. When his students saw it coming, they recited it along with him.

"Barbara! Barbara!"

It was Jenny Lavender. She waved at me as she crossed the room. Jenny is a counselor—a timorously cheerful, imperiously compassionate woman.

"You're not busy?" she said.

"Not yet."

"Oh, good," she cooed, and she beamed at me,

"What do you want, Jenny?"

She blinked. Then her face lit up. "Oh, it's confidential," she said, stepping closer.

Priscilla Wentworth joined us. I introduced them.

Jenny assured Pris that she would love teaching at Pershing. "We're like a family, If you need to talk, if there's anything troubling you..."

I touched her arm. "You wanted to tell me something, Jenny."

"I did? About what? Oh, yes! Yes."

We all leaned closer.

"Kiesha Johnson. You had her last year. She needs some advice and..."

"Advice? About what?"

"She's too young to foreclose her options, because she's basically bright, and..."

"Oh, God," I said. "Stop. I am not the person to do this."

"Oh, but she speaks so highly of you."

"She's pregnant!" blurted Priscilla, catching on.

"It's her decision," said Jenny, "but we have to…you know. I mean, when she's older—a better mother. If she…uh. I'm sure I can get her a basketball scholarship."

"You do that," I said, edging away.

Extending her hand, Jenny talked faster.

"I can't, Jenny. I just can't." I turned, intending to ask Shirley to see to it that Wentworth was reassigned to Yavorov, but she was chatting with her violets.

"Who's been giving ums extra wa-wa, mmm?"

Most of the time, Shirley is the person to see when you want something done at Pershing, but this, I realized, was not something she could do. I would have to talk to Windmuller. I hesitated, but then I was seized by a perverse determination to get this one thing right. This was going to be my last year of teaching and, by God, I was not-not-NOT going to spend six weeks supervising a practice teacher!

Chapter 3

I crossed the hall and knocked on Arnold's door. No answer. I tried the knob. "Hello," I said, stepping inside. The chair behind his desk seemed empty. But he was just bent over. Up he popped

"You didn't knock!"

"Excuse me, Dr. Windmuller, but isn't that student teacher supposed to be ..."

He bent over and disappeared again.

"Sir, didn't we agree that Mrs. Yavorov would be the one who..."

"She's a minority," he called, from below his desk.

"A minority!" I protested. "What's that got to do with it?"

"Calm down, Barbara," he said, sitting up. "Stella simply brought to my attention that the last three practice teachers have all been supervised by minorities."

"Is Romanian a minority? Is that what you're telling me?"

"Romanian?" he replied, puzzled. "Stella is a Native American!"

"What? Since when? What tribe?"

"Don't let's quibble. You're beating a dead stick. Now, the reason I asked you to come see me is about the Coleman Award."

Abigail Coleman taught Latin and English at Pershing for 30 years, from 1924, the year it opened, to 1954. And every year at the awards assembly she gave a hundred dollars to a student who loved to read. The idea was that he or she would use the money to start a personal library. Abby was long gone when I started teaching, but an old timer told me the faculty called it the Abigail's Pet Award.

After Abby retired, she continuing to provide money for the prize, and after she died, her lawyer informed the school that a trust would provide money in perpetuity, but with two stipulations, that the chairman of the English department be solely responsible for selecting the recipient, and that the award continue to be given solely for loving to read.

"Now, look, Barb. According to a rumor assimilated to me, you don't think we have a student who deserves the Coleman award this year."

He smiled to show this couldn't possibly be true.

I said nothing.

"Oh, Miss Butler, come, come. There are hundreds of very deserving poor students out there. We are a very average institution, so excellence has to be present."

Again, I said nothing.

He raised his voice. "It's a statistical fact! You've heard of the Bell Curve? What about Eddy Clambering?"

"He doesn't read. He's a computer freak."

"A what? A what? Miss Butler, we don't call our students 'freaks.' Are you aware of his record? Not that I'm dictating, but I'm told he's a possible Ivy Leaguer. A feather in our caps, eh? But Jenny says he needs a boost to get him admitted. Now what I want is a list of the students you are considering for the award. We'll go over them together, and ..."

"I decide."

"I'm tired of this, Miss Butler! You aren't the only thing on my plate, you know. Personalismo was all right in the past, but ours is a more complicated world. Don't be afraid to ask for help, Miss Butler. That's how we broaden our horizons and identify the neglected who are the backbone of the future, right? I'm with you there, Miss Butler, one hundred percent."

Listening to him almost always sent me into a semi-trance, but when he stopped talking, I roused myself and said, "If I give that award to anyone this year, it will be to Immaculata Saperstein."

"Who? Where's she going?"

"She's not."

"Not going to college? Why give her the award?"

"At least she reads—one book anyway."

"What book?"

"The Bible."

"That's not a book! You can't count that. Does she bring it to school? We could be sued. Look, Miss Butler—Barbara—if that award isn't awarded ..."

He walked to the radiator, and draped his wet socks on it. Then, smiling, he turned to face me. "Look here," he said.

I was. At his feet. He was barefoot.

"If we don't award that award, they'll say we're elitists. Times have changed, Barb. We have to center down over a diverse spectrum, and put the focus where it belongs. The real world. That's our job! We have to prepare them for it!"

He beamed. Then, realizing I was not persuaded, he scowled.

"It's not your money, Miss Butler!"

Red faced, he trotted back to his desk, jerked open a side drawer, and looked down into it.

When he looked up, he was grinning coyly. "Be prepared," he said, lifting out a pair of argyle socks. "That's the Boy Scout motto." Then, sitting down, he lifted his left foot over his right knee and grunted as he tugged on a sock. "I was an Eagle, you know."

"Uh, Dr. Windmuller..."

"Wonderful feeling—being prepared," he repeated, looking down into the open drawer. Then, smiling smugly, he closed it.

Later I would remember that smile.

Drawing myself up, I was ready to make a dramatic, angry exit.

"Wait!" he said, interrupting my timing. He shuffled some papers. Then, having demonstrated his authority, he waved me away. "Never mind. We'll talk later. Run along now or you'll be late."

I wanted to say something snotty but couldn't think of anything he would "get." So I turned to leave but into the room rushed Dr. Justin Sweet.

We collided. He stammered, "Sorry-sorry-sorry." Then, realizing who he'd run into, he spread his arms exclaiming, "You—the very person I need to talk to."

Sweet is one of our two assistant principals—the one in charge of scheduling and supplies. A few years ago, he took a six-week summer course in Transactional Analysis, grew a beard, and decided he was a psychiatrist. Then he started inviting people to stop by his office for "chats." I was asked a lot.

When I pressed the top of my blouse flat, he looked up and said, "Didimo DeVoto."

"What about him?"

"We've had to transfer him to your first period."

"Oh, no! That's my biggest class. It's too late to be transferring students!"

He wiggled apologetically. "I had to redo his entire schedule. I never worked so hard in my life."

"Is this the Harmon thing?" asked Windmuller coming up behind me.

Sweet grunted affirmatively.

Windmuller grunted inquiringly.

Sweet grunted, optimistically.

Windmuller grunted, approvingly.

"What's Vernon Harmon got to do with this?" I demanded, trying to interrupt their imitation of a tennis match.

Ignoring me, Windmuller said, "I want the complete let down on this."

I asked again, louder, "What's Vernon got to do with this?"

The buzzer buzzed!

"First period!" bellowed Windmuller. "And where are we, Miss B.? Not in our classroom, I see!" He made pistols of his fingers and working his thumbs pretended to shoot me, "You're late, Miss B.! Late! Late-late-late!"

Chapter 4

I went back to the main office, collected Wentworth, and led her upstairs. There weren't any students in front of my classroom, which meant one of the boys had used a credit card or a knife to unlock the door. Windmuller kept promising to have shields installed but never did. As we entered, the whooping and hollering stopped and grinning boys ambled to their deskchairs—all but Eddy Clambering, who darted to his, opened a book, and pretended he'd been reading all along.

"What's this shit?" inquired Barney, spoiling Eddy's act by jerking the book from his hands and spinning it into a corner.

Eddy guffawed along with the rest, until he noticed me looking at him.

I'd seen what was on the blackboards but was in no hurry to react. I was thinking how strange it was that I still thought of them as "blackboards." They'd been green for years. It was the same with the school "bell." It was already a buzzer when I, myself, was in high school, but people still called it "the bell." The words "school" and "teacher" and "student" didn't mean what they used to mean, either.

Sighing, I turned to the matter at hand. The greenboards were covered with cartoons of pudenda and of nude Asian

20

women. "Chinkee Stinkee" was written under one drawing.
"Wee Bang Wang" beside another. But Nan Wang, instead
of being in tears, was talking to the girl next to her as if nothing had happened,

"Good morning, class," I said. I introduced a very solemn
Ms. Wentworth and suggested that she sit in an empty deskchair. Then I sat down at my desk and stowed my purse and
thermos in the bottom drawer. Looking up, I saw my new
student on the back row.

"Class, we have a new student today, Didimo DeVoto."
As I wrote his name in my roll book, I asked, "Capital 'V'?"

He didn't answer. I didn't care. Once upon a time, I would
have reacted instantly to what was on the boards. I would
have burst into an oration about tolerance and decency. I
would have overwhelmed them with my sincerity and out-
rage. But if I did that now I'd be worn out before lunch. So I
said calmly, "Barney. Eddy. Erase the boards, please." Then
I calmly explained why tormenting Nan Wang was wrong.

Boys smirked. Girls began combing their hair or putting
on make-up. And I just lost it. I let them have it. I castigated
and condemned. I denounced and disparaged.

"I didn't do anything," bleated Eddy.

I laughed him to scorn and turned my back on them to
look outside. It was raining again—getting darker not light-
er. Behind me, someone snickered. I whirled. "Didimo!" I
sang out. "Calling someone a Chink is just as bad as calling
someone a Nigger." And the spirit came upon me. I preached,
prescribed, denounced, exhorted. But when I heard myself
commanding them "to exchange this false life for a true
one," I interrupted my jeremiad to explain that I was quoting Hester Prynne, a character in the book we were "reading"—so to speak.

"How many books you got memorize?" asked Bud Persinos.

Ignoring him, I invoked the names of Martin Luther King and Roger Williams. I saw them silently wondering, "Roger who?" and the spirit left me, leaving me very tired. Silently, I looked at my students. Silently they looked back. I told Scully Trent to share her book with Ms. Wentworth and told everyone to turn to page 46.

Eddy, waving frantically, blurted, "Hey, Miss Butler, my sister, she goes to Wellesley. You heard a that school? Well, she says that test we take for college is like all matching words, so why don't we practice that, huh? Why don't you help us?"

"I am helping you, Eddy. Stories are full of words, hadn't you noticed?"

"Yeah, but why not just give us a list? Why do we hafta read some story?"

"Eddy, we need to learn to see our lives as stories because…"

I heard myself talking as if I were listening to someone else, and she—I—really sounded stupid to myself. Did I see my own life as a story? No. It was just a series of to-do lists: one damn thing after another.

"Wake up, Barney, yer fartin'," said Clarence, fanning the air with his notebook.

"Okay!" I said, slamming a book on my desk to get their attention. "You don't ask why we're reading *The Scarlet Letter,* and I won't ask you if you do. You pretend and I'll pretend. We all pretend and that's called nonfiction."

Nobody taught *The Scarlet Letter* anymore. I certainly would not have been teaching it if there hadn't been a lot of old copies in the bookroom—or if I'd known I would be teaching it in tandem with a practice teacher. But this was my last year, and I was tired of teaching dumbed-down versions of books that had been purged of "hard words" and politically incorrect expressions.

"Rrrr. Eek. Vahroom!"

Wayland O'Connor was making car-chase noises. His arms were folded across his chest. His eyes were shut.

Immaculata looked up from her Bible and eyed him from across the room. She had confided to me that she wanted to be the perfect mother of two perfect children and the perfect wife of a perfect man. She hadn't mentioned Wayland, but he was obviously her current candidate. They used to sit side by side. I had to separate them.

"Now remember, class," I said, "The people in this book are Puritans."

"Plymouth Rock," sang out Darlene.

"No, Darlene, the Pilgrims go with Plymouth Rock," I replied. "The Pilgrims were like the Puritans, but ... "

"Hey, man, what's with all the history?" complained Clarence. "We get enough of that in Tinder's class."

"They believed in witches, right?"

"They believed," I said, "in sin. Now what is sin?"

"When ja be ba-ad," drawled someone and giggled.

Carmen worked her shoulders and do-dahed a few bars of "Bad Girls."

"Retro," sneered Darlene.

"Hey, Barbara, I know some kids who worship Satan."

"Miss B., my aunt's a palmist. That's like a witch, right?"

"Teacher, teacher, that's been proved! Mr. Dogget told us. E.S.P.—y'know that? Well, the Russians have proved it."

"Never mind! Never mind! Wayland, what does guilt mean?"

"Uh, well, like if they catch you, I guess."

"No, class. Guilt is ... " but I couldn't go on. It was hopeless. "Let's take turns reading aloud," I said. "Eddy, you start. Clarence, share your book with Didimo."

"You go to hell," said Didimo, calmly and waited to see what I would do.

Students looked from him to me and back again.

"Didimo," I said—for lack of anything else to say.

"Didimo," he mimicked.

"Didimo," I repeated, trying a different tone.

He stood up and came towards me. I retreated behind my desk and sat down. He picked up a dictionary, opened it and snapped it shut inches from my nose, causing me to flinch and tuck in my chin.

"Sheee," he drawled, smirking at me.

Then he swaggered from the room.

"Is he crazy?" whispered Darlene, then clapped a hand over her mouth and rolled her eyes.

I wrote a note about Didimo, gave it to Sharon Summerhill, and told her to take it to Dr. Sweet. Then I considered what to do. There was no going back to Hawthorne, not that period. I picked up *The Daily Bulletin*. "All right, class," I said in an almost normal voice. "The office wants to know how many of you ride the bus to school? Raise your hands. School bus? City bus? Private four-wheeled vehicles? Non-motorized two wheeled vehicles? I guess that means bicycles. How many of you walk?"

"Hey, I come on skates. That's eight wheels."

"Do I gotta do the same every day?"

I made up numbers. Accuracy was not the point. The people at Central Office just needed numbers. Any numbers. They need numbers the way vampires need blood. When I finished, I once again started reading aloud from the *Bulletin*—but without reading ahead. A lapse on my part. Too late, I heard myself saying: "No girl wearing pants will be photographed at the Honor Society Tea. Mr. Tinder will check all girls at the door."

I looked up, afraid someone might have "gotten it." No one had. I was relieved—but disappointed, too.

The Bulletin could be counted on. If it wasn't girls' pants, it was the Organ Club. ("The Organ Club is seeking new members. See Mr. Harmon for details.") Or it was, "Come to the pep rally. Show your support for our jocks." But nobody ever "got" the *Bulletin*—or anything else. Getting up, I wrote "ambiguity" on the green blackboard. "All right, class, this is your vocabulary word for today."

But, alas, as I told them what it meant, my ever smoldering passion to explain broke into flame. I related "ambiguity" to *The Scarlet Letter*, to Communism, to soybeans as a source of protein. As I rattled on, I saw Wayland wake up. He yawned, stretched, and took off his shoes. Scully Trent whispered to my practice teacher, who giggled as if she were a high school girl herself. Wayland was squinting at the ceiling, and curling his trigger finger as he fired an imaginary gun. "Kuh! Kuh!" he grunted

I wanted to tell him to sit up and put on his damn shoes, but I couldn't stop explaining. "So you see, class, 'Love' is one of the most am-big-u-ous words in the language."

"Yeah," tittered Darlene. "It's makin' a girl I know biguouser ever day."

Jayleen jumped up shouting, "Kiesha my friend," and threw a pencil at Darlene.

Darlene ducked. The pencil hit Nan who grabbed one of Wayland's shoes and was about to throw it when I, coming up behind her, plucked it from her hand and whacked it on Wayland's head.

"Sit down, Nan. Be quiet, Jayleen. Sit up, Wayland. Here. Put it on!"

Eddy was waving his hand. But he didn't wait to be called on. "Miss B., Miss B., 'love'—is it gonna be on our test?"

Boys wigwagged their elbows and made farting sounds with their armpits.

The bell buzzed, ending first period. And suddenly the room was empty, except for me and Priscilla—and Clarence, who was asleep on the back row.

Chapter 5

I tapped out three aspirin for myself and offered the bottle to Priscilla.

She asked if I was taking them for my heart. She said she'd seen on television that aspirin was good for people with bad hearts.

I said yes, for my heart, figuring what difference did a little more misinformation make in a world that was so full of it. Then she said she admired me and was going to tell her ed-psych prof all about my techniques.

"Gosh, that guy—the good looking one. He's crying out for help, isn't he? So what do we do to help him, Barb?"

Students were coming in for second period. I called out, "Ted, leave Vera alone and sit down."

"But, hey, like nobody warned me we'd be doing Hawthorne. I mean, wow! You don't happen to have a study guide for it, do you, like so I can, like, brush up?"

"Duane, get up off the floor. You're old enough to vote. And Ted…SIT DOWN!"

"We gonna do anything today?" he whined.

Ted wore a cap made of flattened and bent beer cans that had been perforated along the edges and sewn together with yarn.

"We gonna see a flick?" asked Billy Herman. "We never get to see a flick in here."

Renata came in, sat down, and tore several sheets of toilet paper from the roll she was carrying. Then she passed the roll over her shoulder to the girl behind her. They blew their noses in unison.

On the back row, Isaiah raised his right hand, pretending he had a question. Actually, he did, but it was not one I could answer—thank God. Turning his head casually as if looking across the room, he sniffed his armpit. In a moment, he would raise his other hand and sniff his other armpit. He did it every day.

His buddy, Lance, scooted his deskchair into a corner so he could rest his elbows on the chalk rails, like a boxer between rounds. He was wearing his favorite T-shirt. It featured a naked woman and the caption: "Eat It Raw."

I had asked Windmuller if I could tell him not to wear it to school. He said no, that it was a free speech issue.

Leon sat down next to Sally, a drummer in a rock band. She was drumming on her thighs, her desk, her books. She batted Leon's head by way of greeting.

Just as the bell buzzed, in rushed Appaloosa and began passing out papers.

"Stop!" I shouted. "Let me see that. What are you passing out?"

"Aw, come on, Barb."

Every time she calls me by my first name, I ask her not to. And every time she is amazed but agrees not to do it. Then she forgets.

"It's my science project," she protested.

"Cynthia," I warned, using my teacher voice.

She winced. Cynthia was just what her parents called her. Her "real" name was Appa—for Appaloosa, the wild and free.

Reluctantly, she handed me one of the papers.

"I just ask like who's a virgin, and if you're not, what age you started. Stuff like that. Nothin' kinky."

I noticed purple stains on my hands. Was my pen leaking?

"I copied my questions out of a *Seventeen* magazine. You gonna say that's dirty?"

I kept looking at my right palm, wondering what the lines meant. Which, for instance, was my love line? The shortest, no doubt. All nonsense, of course. But I kept looking. I was thinking about Mark Miles saying "the guys" thought I was "hot stuff." What did he think of me now? What had he been thinking when he blushed? I was in my twenties when he was in my class. He'd been seventeen or eighteen. How old was he now?

"Hey, Barb, you ain' lis'nun t'me!"

Third period was much like first and second. Fourth was my split period. I supervised a study hall the first half and ate lunch the second.

"Don't you ever eat in the cafeteria?"

"Never."

I told her how to find it, and then I ate my egg salad sandwich in rejuvenating solitude. Next period, fifth, was my "free" period. I was "free," theoretically, to grade papers. But that day I had to go upstairs and inventory the English books in the book room.

The door wasn't locked. That should have alerted me, but, no, I walked right in, studying last year's inventory on my clipboard. Then I heard a moaning. I froze, then stupidly called out, "Hello. Is someone in here?"

When I found her, I asked, "What happened?"—another stupid question. It was perfectly plain what had happened. "Are you all right?" I asked—yet another stupid question, but I couldn't help myself.

As she was pulling on her panties, she said, "He had a gun." She said it quite distinctly, adding (I must have looked frightened), "Don't worry. He's gone."

"What's your name?" The first sensible question I'd asked.

"Jamie."

The halls were empty. I walked her downstairs to the school nurse and went to tell Windmuller. He asked if I was sure. And before I could reply, he asked if I'd checked "the girl's" file.

"Why would I do that?"

"To check her Personality Inventory—to see if she's trust-worthy. This is very disturbing thing you're telling me. What was she doing in there? Did you ask her that? She was sup-posed to be in class. Why wasn't she in class? Don't worry; I'll have Dr. Sweet talk to her."

"Talk to her? "

"Calm yourself, Miss Butler. It won't do any good to go off un-cocked."

I told him that if he didn't call the police I would.

He said I couldn't do that because I didn't have the au-thority.

So I got out the card Mark Miles had given me, and called him. He wasn't there. Whoever answered asked me if I was the principal. I said, "No." Then he asked for the prin-cipal's name and number. Irritated, I said, "The boy had a gun," and hung up.

I went back to the nurse's office. She said Jamie want-ed aspirin.

"Well, give her one."

"It's medication. I need her parents' permission."

So I asked her to give me an aspirin, which I then passed on to Jamie. Not that I thought one aspirin would do her much good, but I wanted to give her something. I also wanted to stay with her, but I couldn't. Sixth period had already started and Priscilla was up there in my room trying to manage my class all by herself. If somebody got hurt while I was gone, I would be in big trouble.

"Settle down, class. Turn to page 46."

As I read aloud, stopping to explain the hard words, I saw Billy Herman scooting around in his deskchair. I had

Billy twice a day, once in a class of junior English and once in a class of senior English. All because of Gladys Mince. For decades Gladys taught five classes of typing. Then last year Arnold gave her four classes of typing and one of English. She failed half the students in her English class.

This year she was back to teaching five classes of typing.

But the kids she'd failed now had to pass two English courses to graduate. Billy was one of them, and I was going to pass him in both, no matter what. If he graduated, he wouldn't be back, and I would not wish another year of Billy on anyone.

Was he ill? I wondered. Moving closer, I saw his hand was in his pocket and, although his lap was shielded by the armrest, I could tell from the expression on his face what he was doing.

I rushed to the far side of the room. "Look here, students! Look over here!" I called, tapping the green board with my chalk.

Finally the bell buzzed. My students surged from the room. I grabbed the folders I was taking home and retrieved my purse and thermos from the bottom drawer of my desk. I wanted to get down to the nurse's office and see Jamie. I didn't know what I could do for her, but, good grief, she'd just been raped.

Priscilla grabbed my arm. She wanted to talk about her lesson plans.

"When can I can take over? Can I start tomorrow? I've got a lesson plan. Of course it's not about *The Scarlet Letter*. How come you're teaching that anyway? Isn't it really old?"

"Um," I said, and she said, "Look, somebody left his shoes."

"I found a bra once," I replied, waiting for her at the door.

"But shouldn't we put them somewhere so the janitor doesn't throw them out?"

I was tired and was thinking about Jamie and Windmuller and of how everything had gone to hell. My thoughts must have showed because Pris stopped making suggestions.

As we entered the main office, Arnold confronted me. "The police are here!" he hissed. "And they want to talk to you! "

"Good."

"'Good!' What do you mean 'good'?"

He tagged along behind me saying, "You can't go around crying wolf without permission. This is going in your permanent record. Do you hear that, Miss Butler? Your permanent record!"

Mark Miles was in Windmuller's office. He nodded to me but didn't say anything. Two uniformed women seemed to be in charge. They made Arnold leave.

I told my story.

"Did you see who did it?"

"Of course not."

"Did you see the gun?"

"She said he had one."

They conferred.

"What's the matter?" I asked.

It turned out that Jamie wouldn't admit she'd been raped, wouldn't go to the hospital to be examined, denied she'd said anything about a gun, and wanted me to mind my own business.

Arnold was waiting outside. He started to scold me again, but Mark interrupted him to say I'd done the right thing.

Arnold's lips tightened; his eyes bulged; his jowls quivered.

"Here's my card. If you notice anything..."

"You already gave me one."

Mark blushed and grinned. "Oh, yeah," he said. Then he added, "Well, look, don't let this make you reluctant to call. That girl—she's pretty scared."

"Who was that?" Arnold demanded as Mark walked away. "He knows you," he declared, indignantly. "He should be talking to me not you! If she says it didn't happen, it didn't happen. I told you, we could handle this in an orderly way—administratively. But you...you knew better. Now she'll be traumatized!"

"Traumatized?"

"Yes, by having to defend herself against false accusations. That man—he practically accused her of lying. And it's your fault. You put her through this by refusing to go through channels. When you don't do that, what happens, eh? What happens? What happens? What happens?"

I pretended not to hear him, but he went on repeating, "What happens?" getting redder and louder. So I finally said, "I don't know. What?"

He took a deep breath, and in an almost normal voice, said, "Chaos, Miss Butler! Chaos!"

Chapter 6

Priscilla was in the main office waiting for me. She knew about Jamie, the police—everything.

"How did you find out?"

My friend, Vernon Harmon (business math), joined us, saying, "Don't be silly, dear. Nobody has any secrets around here."

"Was she really raped?" asked Pris.

"You look awful," said Vern. "What's wrong?"

"Well, for one thing I have no way to get home. My car's in the shop."

"Let me give you a ride."

"I'd be very grateful."

"Don't overdo it, dear. It's embarrassing."

"I can hardly wait to tell my ed-psych teacher about this school. It's got everything! Diversity-plus."

Vern and I looked at her.

"I mean . . . you know, like you've got everybody from a rapist to the daughter of a congressman . . . uh, I mean congressperson."

"Really," Vern lifted his eyebrows.

"Oh, yes. I forget her name—but that girl—the one you had me sit next to first period."

"Scully Trent?"

"That's her. Her mother's in Congress."

"In prison, more likely," said Vern. "I think you'll find a lot of our students live in fantasy-land most of the time."

I was not so certain about Scully Trent. She was different. Was Trent the name of my representative? I had no idea. I made a mental note to check the girl's file.

Vern was saying, "Would one of our esteemed congresspersons send one of their precious congresschildren to a public school? Hah-ha! Ho-ho! Get real. Anyhow, if he or she did do such an extraordinary thing, wouldn't Arnold know about it? And wouldn't he be having a nervous breakdown and alerting us every day to give her A's and see to it she wasn't persecuted by her lowly peers? Yes, yes, and yes. So, class, what have we learned today?"

"Oh, but I do believe her. Hey, see, I mean, well, like, because of the age thing, mainly. I'm not so . . . Like you, you know—older. Her and me, it's like we talk the same language. Know what I mean?"

"How nice," murmured Vern.

Looking at me, he made a face. Then, looking back at Pris, he smiled demurely.

To break up Vern's little theatrical before he said something he'd regret, I asked, "Hey, what's the story on Didimo? Sweet transferred him to my first period this morning."

"Oh, God!"

He staggered back dramatically. Vern is very dramatic.

"They sent him to you? Oh, darling, I am so sorry. So-ho sorry! Don't hate me, please. It was a matter of life or death."

To Pris, he explained, "Didimo and I just don't speak the same language."

Before she could reply, he turned to me and said, "I'm parked in back. I'll drive around and pick you up on the corner. Glad to meet you, Prissy. Bye-bye."

"Why does that man dislike me?" she asked when he was gone.

"He doesn't. Not really. That's just his way. Tomorrow, we'll talk about your lesson plans."

"I'll get him to like me," she vowed.

Chapter 7

"What a day," I said, getting into Vern's car.

"Mine was super."

"What happened?"

"You first. You look awful."

"You've already said that."

"Just being honest, dear."

That's Vern's vanity. If I gain a pound, or get dressed in the dark, or put on my make-up in the car, he is sure to mention it. Not a likeable trait. On the other hand, he was the only person at Pershing I could laugh with.

"I got off to a bad start, and it was third period before I figured out what was wrong."

"I'm waiting."

"Panty hose on backwards."

"Oh, that'll do it."

Something in his voice … But he was saying, "And then you learned you had a practice teacher, and that you had a new student, and you found that girl in the book room, and she told you to butt out, and Windmuller had a tizzy fit. Sounds pretty normal to me."

"Oh, that's not the half of it." I told him about my car catching fire, and old Bill being shot, and Blaine being Saved, and Didimo threatening me in my first period.

"Why are we laughing?" I asked.

"What's the alternative?"

"Do you know Billy Herman?"

"Herm the Germ? Of course. What's he done now?"

I told him.

Laughing, he raised both hands, looked up at the sky through the windshield and asked, "Lord, how can we pass on the torch of civilization when they won't take their hands out of their pockets?"

"I feel better," I said, when I stopped laughing.

"Where do I turn?"

I invited him in for cocoa and cookies, and while I was heating the milk and getting the cookies from the broom closet that my father had remodeled into a narrow pantry, Vern checked out the house.

"This place is huge," he said as he came back into the kitchen.

"Too big, for me. I moved back in after Mother died. Temporarily, I thought. But then my father got sick. So I stayed. Then he died and here I am. My brother wants to sell it, but I can't face moving until school's out. Okay, so what was so super about your day? You weren't Saved, were you?"

"Oh, dear, I shouldn't have mentioned it. It's a super secret. I'd love to tell you, but … Oh, no, I just can't."

"Has it got something to do with money? Am I cold or hot?"

"Cold. But I'm not playing."

"Does it have to do with ... a student."

"I can match your story about Herm the Germ. Do you know DeeDee Truscot? No? Well, count your blessings. Every day she starts my fourth period by asking for a restroom pass. Well, last Friday, I said no. Don't know why. Just did. So she says, 'I always goes this period.' 'Sit down, DeeDee,' I say. A minute later she calls out, 'All right!' And announces to God and everybody that she's just peed in her pants."

"Good grief! What did you do?"

"Do? What's to do? Out she flounces, and I take a peek. She wasn't kidding!"

"Oh, God!"

"Well, I learned my lesson. From now on, whatever DeeDee wants, DeeDee gets. Yes, indeedy. Including permission to go to the john and smoke the substance of her choice whenever she chooses. Obviously, she needs to smoke dope, and our job is to meet their needs, right?"

We sipped our cocoa and nibbled our cookies.

Inspired, I blurted, "Didimo. It has to do with Didimo."

"Ooo! Red hot! Flaming. Okay, I'll talk, but you can't tell anyone! Not a single-ingle syllable. As it turns out I have something in common with DeeDee."

"A weak bladder?"

"No, no. Boot Vum now on Vahtefer Vernon Vantts, Vernon gets, yah."

Vern is always doing accents.

"You see, I never take papers home. So I stayed late last Friday to grade some tests. On my way out of the building, I go by the main office. It's empty. Even Shirl is gone, which presents me with a temptation to, yes, I admit it, to snoop. And guess what I found. Our beloved Dr. Sweet. And what was our esteemed vice, er, up to? Actually he was just sitting. Yes, but with his trou around his ankles, and that office assistant ..."

He could see I didn't understand, which delighted him.

"Think about it, dear. She was on her knees, and she wasn't praying. You know the one. Long hair. Dimples. Costume jewelry. Very accommodating."

"I don't believe it!" I said, finally understanding. But I did believe it. It was all too believable.

"She didn't see me, of course, and I didn't tarry at the scene of the, ah, impropriety. But I hung around and a while later Sweety and I had a little heart to heart. When I mentioned my problem with Didimo, he very kindly offered to remove the wretch from my class. But I never dreamed he would send him to you. Now take my advice. That boy's not normal. Keep a record of everything he does. Start a file. Complain about him every day. Who knows, maybe they'll transfer him before he kills you."

"Right," I said, but I silently discounted his warning. Didimo was a problem, yes—a serious one—but Vern always exaggerates. "So what happened between you two?"

He couldn't reply because he had just taken a bite of cookie. Then his eyes bulged. He made gagging noises, and slowly waved the cup he was holding back and forth, trying not to spill his cocoa, as he struggled with something.

"Vern, what is it?"

He began coughing, polite, muted, little coughs. But tears were streaming down both his cheeks.

I jumped up—"Here."—and offered him water.

He stood up, too, but slowly, carefully lowering the cup he had been waving every time he coughed. But just then, my cat leaped from the chair where she'd been napping and streaked for the door.

Startled, Vern threw his cup in the air and began coughing great, stentorian, awful, racking coughs, each of them followed by gaspings and wheezings. He clutched his throat, tipped over his chair, tripped over it, and almost fell but managed to stay upright by hopping backward on one leg like a dancing Cossack.

I screamed.

He disappeared—most of him—into the remodeled broom closet, the door of which I had failed to close.

"Vern! Vern!"

I looked down at him. He was jammed into the narrow space, his shoulders hunched around his ears.

I tried to help him up, but he shook his head. He made faces, testing his ability to swallow. When he nodded, I pulled him up and led him back to the table and put a glass of water in front of him.

"Crumb," he croaked, pointing to his throat. "Like broken glass."

"Look at your pants,"

Cocoa was all over them, from the belt down.

"Come," I ordered and led him upstairs. "I've got a pair of sweat pants you can use." But on the way up, I realized my sweats were in the closet in my parents' bedroom, which I was now using as a studio. Vern didn't know about my painting and I didn't know if I wanted him to know. Sure, my pictures were on walls all over the house, but he never mentioned them. Who looks at paintings anymore? Anyhow, I led him to my brother's old bedroom instead which I was now using as my bedroom because I was storing my finished paintings in my own old bedroom. (When I first came back home, I moved into my old bedroom, naturally, and slept in my old bed. I didn't like it. Made me feel like I was growing backwards.)

I left Vern sitting on my bed while I went to get him a pair of my sweats—a pair that I hadn't wiped my hands on while I was painting.

"Here. You can change in the…" I was going to say "bathroom." But he was already down to his underwear, which consisted of panties, pantyhose, and a peach camisole top.

Hugging himself and looking modestly to one side, he slanted a look at me as he murmured, "Surpised?"

Well, I was and I wasn't, so I giggled. "Not really," I said.

He minced over to my closet, took out a dress, and slithered into it.

"Not bad, huh?" he asked, sashaying about.

Throwing himself on my bed, he posed like a centerfold. "Would Windmuller object if I was in *Playboy*? Don't I have a right to express myself?"

"Here!" I called, throwing him another dress. "Try this one."

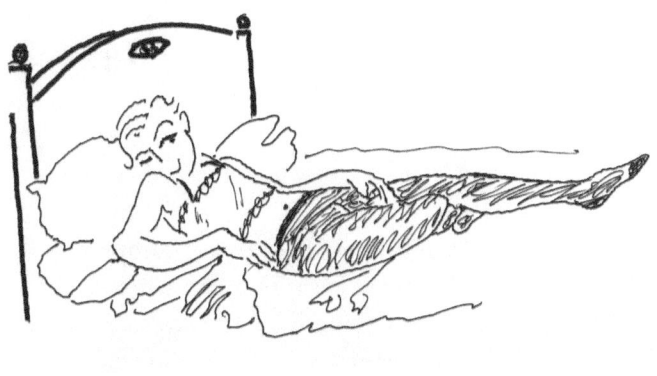

My phone rang, interrupting our playtime.

"Hi, Spence. Fine. How are you?" I said and saw Vern pick up a book from my desk.

"Okay, Spence. Do you know his name? Right. I'll check and call her. Bye."

I dashed across the room and tried to pull the book away from Vern.

As we struggled, he read its title aloud. *"Prayers for All Seasons.* Why don't you want me to read it?'

I let go. I didn't care if he read it. I just didn't like him being so damn nosy. "It was my mother's book," I said.

"Really? I've got a copy signed by the author."

"You...?"

"Do you go to church? Come to mine sometime."

"Yours? You go to church?"

"Well, really, dear, I'm one of God's children, like everyone else. Is this Spence your boyfriend?"

I glared at him.

He cringed comically. "I know. None of my business."

"That's right."

"But is he?"

I gave up. "He's my brother. I'm too old for boyfriends. Do you know a boy called 'Radio'?"

"Should I?"

"He has a band. Amanda—She's my brother's wife. She works for C.T. Denbow and..."

"I've seen their building. What kind of company is it?"

"Who knows? Anyhow, Desmond Birdwhistle—he's its president or chairman or something and she's his executive assistant. Well, his daughter heard this Radio person's band somewhere and wants him to play for her New Year's Eve party. But she goes to a private school and doesn't know how to contact him—or doesn't want to bother. So she asks Daddy. Daddy doesn't want to bother, either, so he tells his executive assistant to find out how to book this kid, and since Amanda knows I teach in a public school, she asks her husband, my brother, to ask me to find out about him. Got it?"

"How come *she* didn't ask you herself?"

Vern is amazingly quick sometimes.

I shrugged, and he didn't press it. Instead he asked, "Does this 'Radio' person go to Pershing?"

"I don't know but one of my kids will know where to find him. They can't read or write but they know all about bands."

Vern was looking at me.

"Don't look at me like that—like I'm a thing."

"You know what you need?"

"To win the Publisher's Clearing House?"

"To do more with your eyes. Come. Sit. I used to be a demonstrator, you know,"

"I don't believe that."

"Tilt. Good. Hold it."

While he studied my images in the three mirrors of my vanity, he said, "You must have driven by my church a million times. It's at Seventy-Fourth on Landis. I'm sure you've seen it. Have you ever tried mauve?"

Before I could reply, he had spread out my make-up on my vanity and was doing things to my eyes.

"There's a girl named Eye-Shadow in the Bible, did you know that?"

I couldn't say anything because he was working on my lips.

"Yes, one of Job's daughters. Now, if you come, don't expect much from our preacher—the Reverend Larry. He looks like a preacher, I'll give him that, but if Lare were a mathematician, two and two would equal whatever he felt they equaled. My suggestion is that you rig up something that looks like a hearing aid and listen to music while he's preaching. When he shuts up, you can turn it off and listen to some real music. We have a marvelous choir. A marvelous organ. And our organist ... "

"And who would that be?" I asked, barely moving my pursed lips in order not to disturb whatever he was doing to me. Actually, I had a pretty good idea who it was.

"Who else?" he replied with a little curtsey. "But if you come, it's Fern."

My eyebrows went up, but otherwise I held still. He was applying blush. When he stopped, I asked, "Doesn't anyone suspect?" I was smiling broadly now, believing in spite of myself what I simply could not believe. "What happened to honest Vern, 'the man who always tells the truth?'"

"What's not honest about it?"

"Well, they think you're a woman!"

"Sometimes I am," he replied, preening.

"You're too much, Vern," I said and quoted Milton, "'Lo, a spirit walks among us.'"

"A spirit?" he inquired archly.

"'For Spirits when they please, / Can either sex assume, or both so...' I forget the rest."

"Oh, I like that."

"Paradise Lost."

"Too bad. Who won? What are we talking about?"

"A poem. You know. 'Paradise Lost.' I wrote my master's thesis on it."

"Well, snooty-poo. I majored in education. And my thesis was on how traditional arithmetic undermines the poor dears' self-esteem, so there."

But he didn't really care because before I could answer, he squeezed my chin, turned my face towards the mirror, and put his cheek next to mine. We gazed together at our glassy essences.

"Nice eyes, darling. See how much bigger I've made them?"

Chapter 8

Vern took off my clothes—not my clothes that were on me, my clothes that were on him! He put his shirt back on and tucked it into my sweat pants. He looked okay, if you didn't look to close. I told him he would probably start a new fashion trend: bow tie, sport coat, and sweats.

He promised to pick me up the next day on his way to school, and I waved him goodbye from my front porch. Back inside, I said aloud, "Okay, let's get to work." But I didn't. I turned on the TV. "Nebraska!" screeched the image of a woman, who appeared from nowhere. "R-R-RIGHT!" shouted the image of a man. "And here's eight HUNdred dollars to make your daREAMS come taRUE!"

They seemed like people from another world. Was there another world? Were my parents there? "You have work to do," I told myself. "Work, work, work to do."

I fixed a plate of leftovers, took it upstairs, sat down at my desk, and started to do my students' mid-term grades. People, I told myself, are more complicated than numbers.

Fairness required flexibility. So I altered and refigured their so-called "objective" grades until I was satisfied that each grade reflected an approximate balance between each student's effort, achievement, and ability, in the light of—God, help me!—his or her "needs and expectations."

For instance, did Nelly deserve a "B"? Or was I giving her one just because I liked her? Could Darlene graduate with a "C"? Oh, but she would be crushed if she didn't get as good a grade as Carmen got. Also, I had to live with her for a-whole-nother semester. There was that to consider. But if I gave her a "C," shouldn't Lance get a "B"?

When I started teaching, I was sure I could show my students how to write decent prose and appreciate literature. I soon realized neither of these skills is teachable. "Learnable," yes, but not teachable. Student themes that I admired were not admired by my fellow teachers. This confused and embittered those students who cared about their grades—not all that many, fortunately. I also realized early on that there was no way to evaluate what a student "got out of" a book. I couldn't even be sure they read the books I assigned. When I was a student I myself used to skim the boring books my teachers assigned and pick out the bits that would be on a test. It's a useful skill, but it's not "reading."

Learning to write well is like learning to dress well; it depends on your image of yourself, which depends on whom you admire and whom you would like to admire you. In other words, it involves a degree of intimacy that no teacher can achieve with 130 students she knows nothing about and sees only forty minutes a day if they all come to class, which they do not. So not long after I started teaching, I lapsed into a condition of detached indifference to my profession and saved my energy for my avocation.

Nevertheless, there were certain professional tasks I had to perform. The worst was to fill out my students' P.I.'s—their Personality Inventories. Once, long ago, I told the counselors the forms were stupid—were examples of pseudo-science. They didn't understand what I was talking about. (I wasn't speaking their language.) What is more, I wasn't "being nice." That's what Jenny told me. So I stopped complaining. It was easier to just fill out the damn forms.

According to the forms, each student has ten "personality characteristics"—things like Intellectual Ability, Effort, Motivation, Leadership, Appearance, Integrity, and so on. Each characteristic has five possible ratings: Extremely Poor, Poor, Average, Above Average, and Extremely High. Okay, what did any of that crap mean? Take "Extremely Poor Intellectual Ability." It was defined as "Dull: grasps ideas only with great difficulty." Oh, thank you, sir. Now would you mind telling me what the hell *that* means?

And each of the ten Personality Characteristics had a number: -1, 0, +1, +2, and +3. That was so we could "add up" a student's personality. That made it "scientific." I had 130 students. If I'd filled out those forms conscientiously, giving each one even a moment's thought, I would have spent weeks on those stupid forms. So I rated everyone average, except Didimo and Billy Herman.

When I finished the Inventories, I went down the hall to my studio—that is to say, to my parents' old bedroom. I didn't turn on the light. Enough came from the light in the hall. I sat in Dad's old chair and gazed at the shadowy unfinished painting on my easel and at the shadowy unfinished paintings propped against the walls. My "precious rubbish."

Recently, I had been doing big faces. Big eyes, twisted features. Visual equivalents of my twisted brain, maybe. I think those paintings saved my life—helped save it, anyhow. But I'm getting ahead of myself.

I never wanted "to be an Artist with a capital 'A.'" The ones I've met have irritated me. I just wanted to paint—to make pictures. When I'm painting, I feel like I'm outside time. At least I'm not aware of it. And when I stop I'm clean—refreshed.

My mother thought I should teach art. But teaching art—oh, God, that would have really depressed me! But I needed to teach something because teachers are the only people who get three-month vacations, and I wanted three months off so I could paint.

My brother keeps wanting me to sell my pictures. He says if I sold them, all the work I put into them would "make sense—dollars and cents." I ignore him, and that's okay. Spence loves me.

I got up and wandered about the room. The house was too big—too empty. My life was empty, too. And my future was scary. I didn't look forward to growing old alone. All at once I found myself rushing down the stairs, switching on lights as I went. My reflection slipped through the mirror on the landing; my shadow slid down the wall and flitted across the living room (where some celebrity on the TV was chummily addressing an imaginary audience). Trailing my right hand across the piano, I caused a flutter of noise and saw my image flash inside the mirror over the buffet.

I put some cocoa, sugar, and a little water in a pan, heated it, and mashed it up with the bottom of a spoon. Then I poured in a cup of milk, stirred it a couple of times, and left it on the stove, while I dropped a slice of bread into the toaster. Noticing my distorted reflection looking back at me from inside the toaster's shiny, slightly curved outside, I saw an intriguing resemblance to the distorted faces I had been painting. So I put my elbows on the counter close to the toaster and cupped my chin in my hands and studied what I saw. I hooked my little fingers into the corners of my mouth and pulled it wide. I stuck out my tongue. I used my index fingers to slant my eyes. I expanded my nostrils and drew my lips back from my teeth and...and then I smelled scorched milk!

Whirling around, I grabbed the smoking pan of cocoa, put it in the sink, turned on a faucet, and then jumped back from the spout of steam that shot up, somersaulting against the ceiling. I started to relax. Then I smelled smoke! My toast was burning! I tried to get it to pop up, but it was stuck.

So I opened the back door and using dishtowels to protect my hands, I threw the damn toaster out into the back yard. By this time smoke was everywhere. It was cold outside but I left the door open, ran cold water over my fingers, and went to bed.

I didn't sleep well. I dreamed someone was yelling at me but I couldn't hear him.

Chapter 9

O n our way to school, I told Vern about scorching the milk and throwing out the toaster. I wanted him to sympathize with poor me.

But all he did was sniff and say he was afraid he was catching a cold.

I punched on his radio. Bing Crosby was in the middle of "White Christmas."

"Not already!" I protested.

"Aren't you looking forward to our Savior's birthday, dear? Think of the weird original arrangements of old carols, the headaches, the quarrels, the financial devastation. Hark, the herald angels sing!"

Without a pause, but in a completely different tone, he asked if I'd seen the paper.

"I don't take the paper."

"Don't take the paper! But you miss all the fun. 'Turmoil in the Schools,' that was the headline this morning. One of their intrepid reporters discovered ... Guess what? That high school principals fail to report all the violent 'incidents' that take place in their schools. Astonishing, no? Who'd a thought it?'"

"I don't think that's funny."

"Get real, dear. They're going to pay a consultant to define violence for the principals. Haven't you always wondered what it meant? Then they'll know what to report. And the Superintendent said he would 'develop strategies for better communication.' Aren't you relieved?"

He looked at me archly, and I grinned in spite of myself. Not until he parked and we were walking towards the building did we sober up and put on our game faces.

Sitting at my desk, copying the names of the absent students from my roll book to my Hourly Absent/Tardy Report, I looked up and saw Scully Trent slinking over to talk to Priscilla Wentworth. Was she really a congressman's daughter? I reminded myself to find out the name of my congressman.

Priscilla was pouting because I'd told her she was going to have to wait to take over my classes until they finished the work I'd already given them. Didimo was absent, which was a relief. So was Immaculata which was unusual. "Wayland, is Immaculata sick?" I asked, handing the Absent/Tardy report to Carmen, who would post it on the outside of the classroom door for an office assistant to pick up.

"Wake up, Wayland. I asked you a question."

"I, uh, I'm not sure."

While Carmen was out in the hall, I passed back the paragraphs I'd graded. And when she returned, I explained—again—about plagiarism.

"Yeah, but not if you change a word in each sentence," protested Eddy.

"Yes, even if you change a word in each sentence."

A moment later, without raising his hand, he blurted, "I guess my speech for the speech contest is plagiarized then. You're a judge of that, right?"

I praised him for his honesty.

Surprised, he basked in my approval.

First period was uneventful.

Second was almost more than I could bear. Herm the Germ came late without a pink pass. I re-did my roll book and my Hourly Absent/Tardy report. Then Ted arrived, wearing his cap of flattened beer cans. He had a pass, but I still had to re-do my roll book, and this time I had to send a student to the office to retrieve my Hourly Report, which had already been collected. I also made out a detention form for Herm for being tardy. He would never serve it. There weren't enough Saturdays in a century for Herm to serve all his detentions, but I had to do something about him, didn't I?

A student assistant arrived with a note from Dr. Pisapus, the attendance counselor. He wanted me to know that there was "an inconsistency "on my fifth period A/T Report for last Friday and that I should come to his office as soon as possible "to verify my error."

I countersigned the girl's pass and told her, "You tell Pisapus I don't have a fifth period."

Then Appaloosa asked for a restroom pass, and Lance and Isaiah asked for passes to the Senior Lounge to use during their study hall. I wrote a pass for Appa, but I couldn't find my Senior Lounge passes.

"'Snot fair!" the boys protested.

The Senior Lounge is a room where seniors who have not been on detention for a month can relax from the rigors of getting an education. In plain English, they can smoke in there. The administration justified this on the same grounds that they justified distributing condoms: They said, "They're going to do it anyway," and "We don't want them sneaking around, do we?"

Actually, I do. I approve of hypocrisy. It shows something still matters.

Another student assistant arrived. She had a note from Sweet. He said he had "routed" my note about Didimo to Dr. Mossman. He's the other assistant principal—the one in charge of discipline.

"Students! If you don't be quiet, I'm going to give you a test."

"Communist! Communist!" hissed Herm.

I countersigned the student assistant's pass and sent her off. But before I could restart the class, another student assistant arrived. This one had a note from Ms. Riddle, the librarian. She said her records showed Renata Maddingly had checked out three copies of *Glamour* last semester and failed to return them. She wanted Renata sent to the library at once.

I wrote a hall pass for Renata and sent her off.

"All right," I said, "today's the day your proverbs are due. Who's got one? Duane?"

"Uh, well, 'You can't tell a horse by its cover.'"

"Hey, Miss Butler, I got one. 'Don't count your eggs before they hatch.'"

"Wait!" I said. "That doesn't make sense. And, Duane, now that I think of it, yours doesn't either. You've got 'You can't tell a book by its cover' mixed up with 'That's a horse of a different color.'"

"Who says?" demanded Duane.

"Makes sense t'me," said Ted.

"All right, Ted, what's it mean?"

"Well, if one hatches, you don't got so many to eat."

"No ... Wait!"

I was confused. Did that make sense?

Rodney shouted, "'A rolling stone gathers no moss.' That means if you keep changin' jobs, you don't get retirement benefits. My mother said so."

"'Money is the fruit of all evil,'" someone called out.

"Wait! Wait!" I shouted.

A girl strolled in the room with a note from Jenny Lavender asking for Duane.

"What's this about, Duane?"

"Aw, she wants I should go to college, but I'm goin' t' California."

Renata and Appaloosa came back just as the office assistant went out with Duane, and as he passed them he did something that made all the boys laugh. I ignored it.

"Now about these proverbs."

The student assistant who'd come for Duane came back in, saying, "You forgot to sign my pass, Miss Butler."

As I signed it, Appaloosa called out, "Hey, I got one. 'A journey of a thousand miles stops at the first step.'"

"Where'd you get that, Appa?"

"Copied it from a book."

"Well, you copied it wrong."

"Aw, it counts, don't it? 'S close enough isn't? Don't be mean, Miss B."

"I'm not being mean! What's it mean?"

"Uh? Give up, I guess."

At that point little Dr. Ralph Treadway, one of our counselors, marched into my room followed by Dr. T.K. (Monster Man) Mossman.

The boys slouched and affected indifference.

Doris put away her nail polish.

"We would like to borrow Billy Herman, Miss Butler," rumbled Mossman.

"Certainly, Dr. Mossman," said I, "but could I have a word with you first."

I told Priscilla to take charge and continue the discussion of proverbs. Then I went out to the hall with the two men.

"Why now?" I demanded. "I've had a thousand interruptions this period."

They exchanged looks. I could tell what they were thinking. Here it was again. The old female emotionalism. The old tendency to exaggerate.

Treadway explained, "It's to stop all the inner-ruptions. This kid—he's tardy all the time. You aware of that? Pisapus gimme the numbers on him. I updated T.K. So here we are. We gotta do somethin'."

Mossman harrumphed and declared, "The administration cannot always arrange things for the convenience of the individual teacher."

That reminded me. "Did you get my note about Didimo DeVoto?"

"I get a great many notes, Miss Butler. What was it about?"

"He told me to go to hell and walked out of my class."

Treadway looked at Mossman. "Is that the kid that's on probation?'

"Probation? Real probation? Probation ordered by a court? Why wasn't I told?"

Regretting his indiscretion, Treadway glanced apprehensively at Mossman, who explained, "It's policy, Miss Butler. So they won't feel their teachers are discriminating against them."

"They? Them? How many of my students are on probation?"

"How was it that you lost control of the DeVoto boy?" demanded Mossman.

"Forget it. I'm sorry I brought it up."

"We can't just forget things, Miss Butler. This is a serious matter."

There was a loud noise. We looked towards it. Two boys dashed from the side hall and disappeared down the south stairs.

Mossman frowned and unbuttoned his coat,

Treadway scratched his crotch and looked to his superior for guidance.

I glared at them both.

Mossman buttoned his coat. "No need to panic, Miss Butler."

He waited a moment longer, then he strolled off to investigate.

Before Treadway could follow him, I grabbed his arm, "What's he on probation for?"

"Who?"

"Didimo."

"Oh, he's not the one. I was thinking of the Delany kid."

Walking back into my room, I commanded, "Stop it!"

"What's the matter?" said Pris.

Seeing they were caught, one of the boys on the back row called out, "Hey, it's Super Ball Sunday on CBS!"

"Pick those up," I commanded.

"Why me? I never do nothin'. You say so yourself."

Lance and Isaiah were already crawling around on the floor picking up the balls of wadded paper—but they were also continuing their game by tossing the balls at the wastebasket.

"Oh, bullcrap," muttered Lance, missing a shot.

Feeling my glare, he looked up and explained, "'At'snotta bad word, Miss B. Now 'f Ida said bullsheee … That of been a bad word."

Appaloosa was waving at me. "What is it, Appaloosa?"

"Where'd j'getcher shoes, Miss B.? They're really cool."

And from between her cherry lips slipped a little pink balloon.

I was so distracted by its steady expansion, I couldn't remember what she'd asked me. It didn't matter though, because her bubble burst; the "bell" buzzed and the period was over.

I told myself that I didn't believe in omens or symbolic foreshadowings. That kind of stuff was for "literature," not life. But when that bubble popped it was like … Well, I remember having this uncanny feeling that before long my life was going to pop, too.

Major Characters who appear after Chapter 9

Chapter 10

The counselors were giving the seniors an aptitude test in the auditorium during third period, so I took Pris to the faculty lounge.

"Bring those vocabulary tests. We'll grade them down there."

But we left too soon. The halls were still crowded with students changing classes. A boy bumped into Pris and sent her staggering.

"Excuse me!" I shouted, sarcastically, but he didn't notice. He was too busy picking up the empty cigarette packages that had spilled from the grocery sack he was carrying.

"Cigarettes!" gasped Pris, cringing and hopping backward even as she was slipping her shoe back on.

"Yeah, for somebody with cancer," the boy explained.

"I beg your pardon?" I said.

He scowled at me.

"We don't understand," I translated.

"No? Well, see, Remora, she got this barrel in her room an' if we collect a million empties, they'll give an iron lung to somebody for free."

"'They'? Who? An 'iron lung'? Wait!"

"Bring yer empties to Room 215," he called back as he hurried away.

"What's he talking about?" asked Pris.

Before I could answer, Max Tinder joined us.

"If they think they're gettin' away with it, they're crazy," he declared.

"Right," I agreed. (I always agree with Max. It's easier.) "Max, this is Priscilla Wentworth. She's a practice teacher. And Pris, this is Max Tinder, our union steward."

"Pris, huh? Hey, solidarity forever."

"Solidarity forever," she repeated, giggling.

As we trooped downstairs, he complained about "the big boys."

"The union sees right through their crap."

"That's good," I said.

"I'm peelin' off," he said, stopping before Windmuller's office. "You tell 'em in the lounge that ol' Max will be along in a minute with the big boy's scalp on his belt."

"We'll tell them, Max."

As we walked on, Pris asked, "What's he so upset about?"

"Who knows?"

At the table in the middle of the room, Clara Dingle (home ec.) was slicing a chocolate cake.

Over in a corner, Phil Sitwell (geography) was reading the *Wall Street Journal.*

And Lyle Doggett (chemistry) was lying on the couch with his eyes shut. Without opening them, he said, "Phil, don't you have a class this period?"

Phil rattled the newspaper to show he was reading faster.

Clara, whose mouth was full, waved a greeting and pointed to the cake.

I introduced Priscilla to the room in general.

Lyle opened his eyes and raised one hand.

Phil peeked over the top of his paper and said, "Hi."

We sat down at the table and I showed Pris how to grade the tests.

"But don't we have a key?"

"I don't use a key."

"But wouldn't it be easier?"

"I suppose."

Between bites of cake, Clara said, "I hear the pregnancy thing for the Johnson girl is for sure. Have you heard that? So who's the father? Any ideas?"

As if he had been cranked, Lyle began his familiar prophecy of the imminent overpopulation of the world, which would be accompanied by mass starvation, epidemics, universal pollution, religious frenzies, and nuclear wars.

"We've got to face reality," he said, gazing at the ceiling.

Clara made a rabbit face at him, then silently offered me a slice of cake.

"No, thank you." And noticing that Pris had given a student credit for "banal" in the sentence, "The Constitution is a 'banal' document," I leaned close and quietly told her we couldn't give credit for that use of "banal." She stiffened and insisted loudly that I was wrong. (So much for my effort to be tactful.) Trotting herself across the room to the big dictionary, she flipped its pages and read aloud: "'boring, devoid of freshness or originality.' Okay, that's the Constitution, isn't it? And down here it says ... Well it says, 'OF ban (see ban 2).' Does that make sense? Anyhow ban 2 says, 'a public proclamation or edict.' That's like the Constitution, right?"

I said firmly, "'Banal' means 'insipid' or 'trite.' Do you think the Constitution is insipid or trite?"

"I don't know, I never read it, but some people might, and since we're like multicultural, we've all got a right to our own language, right? That's what the N.C.T.E. says. I had Garbahj in school. A.A. Garbahj. You don't? Really? He was chairman of N.C.T.E.'s. committee on language development. And he's been on TV because he's the expert on tenth grade vocabulary. I had his seminar, and, see, it's like I have to be me, and you have to be you, so if I use some word or something my way, that's just me being me, and the same goes for you, because otherwise, you know, language gets to be a tool for oppression instead of expression, and that's why we're having this crisis until we get people free to communicate, even if they can't, like, you know, do all old Miss Nitpicky's social codes and password stuff."

"Old Miss Nitpicky?"

She was stricken by the realization that I might be a real-life version of the fabled Nitpicky and immediately tried to apologize: "Aw, gee, gosh, uh, you know what I mean." Squirming, she tented her eyebrows, signaling embarrassment, anguish, and submission.

I went on grading.

She looked woefully at Clara, appealing for help.

Clara wanted to help but didn't understand the problem, so she put a slice of cake on a scrap of wax paper and slid it towards me.

I looked at her. She smiled and nodded, as if we secretly understood each other.

"I'm on a diet," I lied.

"Ooo," groaned Clara and Pris together.

They understood "diet."

Over on the couch, Lyle spoke to the ceiling about how intelligent people could make the world a paradise if only some new plague would reduce the world's population by a third.

"AIDS?" he asked himself rhetorically. "No," he answered himself, "it has to be something that will reduce the number of women in the childbearing age cohort." He paused, then added with scientific sobriety, "Actually, this could be our opportunity to improve the gene pool. That's where genetic engineering comes in."

The door banged open and in barged a red-faced Max Tinder.

"We've GOT to get ORGA-NIZED!" he boomed.

"Have some cake," urged Clara, licking her fingertips.

Max spun a chair around and sat down. Leaning over its back, he slapped the table and said, "Listen! The cops just busted a kid outa Ruby Remora's class. Yeah, so I told old Windbag.

I said, 'This is an OSHA issue!' Kids like that are threats to the safety and health of the workers, right?" Jabbing a finger at me, he shouted, "I'm right, right?"

"What are you talking about?" I asked.

"Here? In school? They arrested a st-student?" stammered Clara.

"What'd they arrest him for?" drawled Lyle.

Max hesitated. He didn't know. But he was a teacher. Teachers know. "Oh, some drug thing. But anyhow, I grabbed my chance to tell old Windbag about my car."

Lowering his newspaper, Sitwell smiled a crooked smile full of crooked, tawny teeth. "Your car?" he said.

"Read your union newsletter, bro," ordered Max. "Last month, a teacher at Southpark Junior High got his tires slit, and a teacher at Central got his spray-painted with the filthiest goddamn crap you ever saw."

"What happened to your car, Max?"

"That's what that S.O.B. Windmuller kept asking. Do we have to wait for something to happen before we act? That's management's position, for Chrissake!"

"It's chocolate," Clara reminded him, licking her fingertips.

Lyle got off the couch and stood behind me, as I graded papers.

"I see you've got Appaloosy,"

"That nut," sputtered Max. "Rocks in her seat. Whinnies? Thinks she's a horse. Listen, when I was a kid, you had your head screwed on or you got your ass kicked. Look at the SAT scores. That proves it."

Pris said her professors said that the SATs were designed for a different era. "Kids today are smart in ways those tests don't measure."

I stacked my vocabulary tests and stood up. I wanted out of there.

Phil Sitwell stood up too, tossing his newspaper on the chair behind him. "It says in there," he said, "that lots of principals keep guns in their desks."

"You're kidding," I said, stopping halfway to the door.

"Not kidding."

"That can't be right," I insisted. picking up his discarded newspaper. "Where is it?"

"Front page."

"This is unbelievable," I said. I felt as if I were confronting a dog with feathers.

"Uh, does that mean they, uh, think teachers should have guns?" asked Clara.

"I've been TELLING you," said Max, scowling as he stuffed cake in his mouth. "It's a PLOT—a plot against labor. And it starts right at the TOP!"

"The top?" I echoed, looking up from the article.

"YES! YES! The big white abode itself! There's a lot of angles to this thing, but they're out to break the union! YES! THAT'S THE ONLY WAY IT MAKES SENSE! They canceled our Scholastic magazines, didn't they? And that's a teaching tool! But as you can see right there the library is still gettin' its precious *Wall Street Journal,* right? And who's that for, huh? THE BIG BOYS, THAT'S WHO. AND THEY DON'T GIVE A DAMN ABOUT US. HOW COME THE KIDS HAVE GUNS BUT WE DON'T?"

"Max, what are you sayin'?" asked Lyle, amused.

"Oh, dear," murmured Clara. "Wouldn't we need to take a workshop first?"

"No, no!" boomed Max. "The point is BAN GUNS. Let's keep our eyes on the ball! SO why haven't they done it? Who's behind it? FOLLOW THE MONEY; THESE THINGS DON'T JUST HAPPEN."

"Careful, Max," drawled Lyle. "I haven't had my CPR

trainin' yet."

Nudging me, Clara asked, "I don't think Dr. Windmuller has a—er, one of those things in his desk. Do you?"

"THAT BASTARD! THAT MORON! HE'D SHOOT HIMSELF IN THE FOOT WITH IT!" shouted Max, addressing the walls, where he was sure that "the administration" had planted listening devices.

Folding the *Journal,* I asked no one in particular, "Has the whole world gone crazy?"

Lyle patted my shoulder and explained, "The problem here's there's just too much of everything—too much information, too many choices, too many people. Did you know the population of India is going to triple in … Where you goin'?"

I'd heard about the population of India from Lyle before.

Chapter 11

The bell buzzed before we got upstairs. Doors opened. Students streamed into the hall. Vern came out of his room and hailed us, "Hello, girls! Ready for our meeting?"

We sheltered from the crowd in the angle of his open door. "Meeting?"

"The speech contest. After school. You're a judge, remember."

"Oh, Lord."

"Is this a requirement?" asked Pris, "Because, after school, there's this guy..."

"Go with your guy."

"Really, is it okay? Really?"

"It's okay," Vern and I chorused.

A boy who had just gone into Vern's classroom came back out and offered him a book.

"What's this, Pete?"

"Foun' it on my desk," he said, listlessly.

"Someone left a book on your desk? Okay, give it to me, and I'll..."

But the boy had been studying the book. He looked up, said, "Uh, 'smine, I guess," and walked back inside.

"Is there a lot of dope in this school?" asked Pris. "Because Mr. Tinder, Max, he said somebody was arrested for it in Miss Remora's class."

"A lot of dopes," said Vern.

I told him about Ruby Remora's campaign to collect a million empty cigarette packages. "She thinks she can turn them in to somebody who will buy an iron lung for somebody with cancer."

"Are you serious? She thinks people with lung cancer are treated in iron lungs?"

"Urban folklore!" I explained.

"What's an iron lung?" asked Pris.

But the bell buzzed, and without a word, Vern ducked into his room, leaving Pris and me in the nearly empty hall.

"Was that the lunch bell?"

I sent her off to the cafeteria. When sixth period started, she still wasn't back. Students rushed into my room totally ignoring me. Some girls were weeping. Other girls huddled around them. Boys conferred in different parts of the room.

"What's going on? Sit down! Sit down!"

"Haven't you heard?"

"Heard what?"

"He killed her."

I was sure I'd misunderstood. "What are you talking about?"

Priscilla rushed in and grabbed my arm. "It's Wayland O'Connor. He's the one!"

"The one what?" I asked, prying her fingers from my arm.

A student called out, "The one who was arrested! He killed her!"

I remembered what Max said about a student being arrested for something having to do with drugs, and told my students they must be confused. It was probably drugs.

They shouted me down. "Drugs? No! Murder! Murder!"

"He was robbin' a 7-Eleven, and he murdered her."

Priscilla grabbed my arm again. "A girl named Saperstein. She's one of ours, too, isn't she? That's what I told everybody. We had them both! It's incredible!"

"Confusion now hath made his masterpiece!" I said, quoting Macduff. (I taught *Macbeth* so many years I had the whole play memorized.)

Sobbing girls testified to Immaculata's sweetness.

Other girls repeated, to each other, "This is horrible. I can't believe it."

The boys wanted to know what kind of gun Wayland used.

"Wait! Stop! Sit down! None of you know that Wayland actually did this!"

They said "everybody" knew.

"He used to work there, but he got fired. So he wanted back at him."

"Stop! Stop it!" I shouted. "Op-open your books to…to…"

"Hey, Miss B., we can't… We just can't!"

I gave up and began playing with paper clips. Should I have seen this coming? Could Immaculata really be dead? Could Wayland really have killed her?

Somebody said, "What I don't get is why. Because he was pretty popular."

Somebody said, "So anybody goes ape has to be a dumbo, right?"

"Well, he's still my friend."

"Well, she was *my* friend."

"Why did he shoot her eyes?"

"Is that right? He shot her eyes?"

"Because if she was looking at him when she died, his face would still be on her eyeballs."

"Oh, that's a crock."

"Nick says Satan did it," said Tyella.

I beckoned for her to my desk. "What's this about Satan?"

"Oh, Nick Specter. You know, who puts out butts on his arms? He says..."

Dupree came up behind her and said, "I knew something bad was going to happen today, because last night our dog started barking at nothing, and my sister's radio went on all by itself."

Wade interrupted. "My aunt sees stuff, you know, like the future. But yesterday she saw something she shouldn't and was blind for two hours. Ask my mother."

Then Priscilla leaned close and whispered, "I know it sounds weird, but yesterday in the paper, my horoscope said..."

After school in the main office, everyone was talking about Wayland.

"Starts right at the top," boomed Max Tinder.

"We're all victims," Dr. Sweet explained, combing his short beard with his fingers. "We all hurt."

Ruby Remora grabbed my arm. "You had her didn't you? Was she breaking up with him, or what?"

"I wasn't prepared for this," said Jenny, sniffling.

Pris wanted to know if I thought we would be on TV.

"What?"

"Well, because we had them both. Have you ever been on TV before?"

"What happened?" asked Gladys Mince.

"This is very troubling," rumbled Lyle Doggett.

Yes, it was. We worked in a little world where grades were adjustable and rapes deniable. But this—this wasn't adjustable or deniable. I sat down at Shirley's desk and heard someone say that Wayland had worn a ski-mask. How did people know these things?

"You're crying," said Jenny, touching my arm. "What's wrong?"

I heard Clara explain, "She had that girl, the one that was killed." But before Jenny could encumber me with comfort, I bounced up, intending to get out—out of that room, out of the school.

Lyle blocked my way. He wanted to tell me about "Y" chromosomes, chemical imbalances, and bad protoplasm.

"Is he a Catholic?" asked Ralph. "Maybe he was abused. That would explain it."

Tinder and Jay Sharp (mechanical drawing) agreed with each other that drugs and television were more likely explanations.

"Oh, the signs were there."

"Plain as your nose."

"He was crying out for help," agreed Jenny.

"Like I say," said Max, "this administration we got in Washington ... "

"He helped me move my desk once," offered Phil Sitwell, not wanting to be left out.

Justin Sweet came over to me and said, "I checked his permanent record. Did you know he was expelled once in elementary school?"

"What?"

"He drew a picture of a gun in his social studies book."

That did it. I pulled myself together and protested, "A picture of a gun? All boys draw pictures of guns. You're telling me his teacher thought a picture of a ... "

"We don't have to think, Miss B.," said Windmuller, who had just come into the room, "We have rules. You'd better get used to it, Barbara. Objectivity, Fairness. No more favoritism. If you get my drift."

"We have to face the facts," murmured Sweet, looking at me sorrowfully.

"Facts be damned," I said. "Wayland didn't do this." And the moment I said it, I knew I was right.

"Oh, Barbara, Barbara, we can't sentimentalize," said Sweet, nearly ecstatic with compassion. "I know how you feel. I feel the same way. This boy is one of our own. We failed him, so we can't desert him. Whether he's guilty or not, he's going to face ... "

Smiling his wan, weak smile of predatory compassion. he waited for me to finish his sentence.

I stared at him. All I could think of was what Vern had told me about this man and the girl with the long hair, dimples, and costume jewelry.

Sweet had to finish his sentence himself: "... a terrific adjustment."

Turning to the other teachers, he said, "There will be a period of ... "

He made a gesture of invitation and encouragement, but no one spoke. So once again he had to finish his sentence himself: "... of very human despondency. I just hope wherever they send him there are some caring professionals who can help him through it."

"We should pray for him," suggested Jenny.

But that was not what Sweet had in mind,

Vern said loudly, "Good idea, Jenny. Don't you think that's a good idea, Dr. Sweet?"

Disconcerted, Sweet said, "It certainly couldn't hurt." And then he winked at me, as if we understood each other.

"It might even help!" observed Vern, who also winked at me as if we understood each other. Then, turning to Jenny, he reminded her that the world wasn't going to stop because of Wayland. "We have a speech contest to judge, remember. Or shall we postpone it on account of tragedy?"

"Oh, we can't! The names of the finalists have to be in tomorrow. If we postpone it, we'll be the only school without a candidate, and Dr. Windmuller will be so embarrassed. Come on. Where's Mr. Tinder? Has anybody seen Mr. Tinder?"

Max was waiting for us in Jenny's office. "Where y'all been? If we don't hurry I'm gonna be late for work."

"We're just getting off work," I said, confused.

"You're getting off, babe-oh. I got a family to support."

Vern asked, "What kind of second job do you have, Max?"

"All I do is work! You been reading about that kid they're givin' a gazillion bucks to play basketball? You judge a civilization by the way it treats its teachers, right? Because we're the ones holdin' things together—the past and the future."

"Think of it," said Vern, glancing at me. "Millions of dollars to a mere boy."

Max removed his feet from Jenny's desk and leaned over it. "It'd be different if they worked for it—climbed the ladder like the rest of us."

"It certainly would," Vern agreed, grinning broadly now. "They're just born with big feet."

"Exactly!" boomed Max, pounding the desk. "Aristocracy, deja vu. Do we want a country where a guy collects millions on account of an accident of birth, or one where what counts is our social worth?"

"Feet," said Jenny. "What about feet?"

"Basketball players, Jenny. They're seven feet tall."

"Oh, I see what you mean," she said doubtfully.

I wanted to shout that Immaculata Saperstein was dead, but I didn't. All I did was tap my stack of papers so that their edges were nice and even.

Jenny passed out the evaluation forms, saying, "I'll read you the rules. The contestants are anonymous. You mark each category fair, good, and … "

"Forget that," growled Max. "Let's hear the tapes!"

Jenny slid a tape into the machine and pressed play: nothing, just hissing.

"I-I don't understand," she stuttered, cringing a little.

"Play number two," growled Max.

"The prr-RICE of LIBerty IS … " shouted a girl's voice. Then a man's voice said, "Hit 'liberty' a little more, hon."

"Next," said Max.

"Oh, I'm so sorry," apologized Jenny. "I've wasted your valuable time, haven't I?"

On the next tape a boy raved about the "indivisible" rights of Americans that existed "because of the sacred document of our forefathers, the Constitution!"

Vern said, "Ugh!"

"But that's all there is," wailed Jenny.

Max said, "Okay, then that last one. He's our winner. I'm outa here."

"Wait," I said. "That was Eddy Clambering. I recognized his voice. He plagiarized his speech. He told me so this morning. He didn't know what plagiarism meant. He thought if he… "

Max interrupted: "Never heard of it until this morning, eh? Well, so you ever heard of ex post facto, eh? That's a wrap. Be seein' ya. Over and out."

"But, but, but…."

Jenny said, "We have to have a winner. How can Dr. Windmuller explain if we're the only school without a representative?"

"And whoever represents us has to be good!" asserted Max. "With this murder thing, this schools' rep is going smash-o, crash-o. Okay, we've got our winner. Bye now."

"Well, Barbara," said Vern, grinning. (He was enjoying this whole thing.) "Since, as you say, the boy didn't know what plagiarism meant until today, maybe we should be, um, flexible."

"But what will he think?" I said.

"Who?" asked Jen.

"The boy! Eddy. About winning. He knows he cheated. I told him so."

"Cheated!" chorused Max and Jenny.

They looked at me like I had spots.

"Such a judgmental word, dear," murmured Vern. "Surely there's another way we can put it."

"Vern, this isn't funny."

He rolled his eyes.

"I can get him a scholarship if he wins," said Jenny. "He makes A's, but he needs extracurriculars."

"He's not making an 'A' in my class," I said.

"Oh, but he always makes A's."

"Listen, gazebos, whatever you decide is hunky dory by me. But this little doggie's gotta git along. Sire-a-nora."

"Have the boy write a new speech," Vern suggested.

"You mean, have another contest?"

I didn't want to believe they were all crazy, because if they were, then nothing I said would ever make sense. And if nothing I said ever made sense, then I would be crazy, too, wouldn't I? Isn't that what it means to be crazy—to be unable to make sense?

"We don't have time," moaned Jenny. "Tomorrow's the last day."

"I've GOT to GO. We agree, right?" said Max, bouncing a little.

"I've got to think about this," I said.

"She'll think about it," simpered Vern.

Jenny walked us down the hall, urging me to remember what a nice boy Eddy was, and, as I stopped to turn up my collar before going outside, she made one last pitch.

"We have to reward honesty, don't we? If we don't show we appreciate it, what reason will he have to ever be honest again?"

Chapter 12

Vern let me off at the gas station where I left my car.

"Hello, I'm Miss Butler. I understand my car is ready?"

I wanted to ask about the man who was shot—Bill—but Blaine wasn't there, and I was having a hard time getting anyone's attention. "Hello, I was told my car is ready."

The young man I addressed was frowning at a rack holding cans of motor oil.

"I telephoned earlier, and I was told that … "

He seized a can of oil and rushed from the room.

I started after him, but, hearing a door shut behind me, I turned and saw an old man stepping from the restroom. He was still tucking his shirt in.

"Do you work here? I've come to pick up my car."

He, too, said nothing, but after buckling his belt and zipping his fly, he pulled a stack of dirty work orders from a drawer and began, laboriously, turning up their corners with a large, dirty finger. After doing this for a moment, he paused, frowned, and looked up at me."Wha'djasay yer name was?"

With that information, he found my work order. I gave him my credit card. He ran it through his machine. I signed the slip. He gave me the receipt.

Then he looked out the window.

"My keys," I inquired sharply.

"In it," he replied, continuing to look out the window.

"In what?"

He finally looked at me but said nothing, and I realized the keys would be in my car.

"Oh," I said, and started for the door. Then I realized I didn't know where my car was and turned around, just in time to see the restroom door closing behind him.

Driving home, I wondered if the men at that place acted like that to everyone? They couldn't, could they—and stay in business? No. So maybe just to women? But, no. That would ruin their business, too. So it was me, wasn't it? Something about me. I was not unaware of my faults. I'm not friendly like my brother. I look at people like I might paint a picture of them or do a cartoon of them. Which of their features should I exaggerate? Is one of their ears bigger than the other? People don't like to be looked at like that. I know this but don't much care.

Feeling sorry for myself, I looked forward to a cup of cocoa, which reminded me that I was out of milk. So I stopped by Kim Soo's convenience store to get some.

On my front porch, hugging my sack of groceries while searching my purse for my key, I heard the phone ringing inside the house.

I panicked.

Foolish, I know, but if I'm in the tub or out in the yard or if I'm painting... That's the worst because chances are I'm not in a good place to stop. Anyhow, if I hear the phone, I assume it's important and if I miss this particular call, something awful will happen or something wonderful won't.

So charging into the house, I raced to the phone, "Hello! Hello!"

And then the letdown. "Oh, hi, Amanda." And thinking I knew what she was going to say, I said, "I'm afraid I forgot all about 'Radio.'"

"Who?"

"The boy you asked Spence to ask me to find. The one who has the band."

But she wasn't calling about Radio. She'd heard about Immaculata.

"Isn't it awful about that girl? She was from your school. Did you know her?"

"I had her in class. The boy, too."

She was thrilled. I wasn't surprised. Amanda has really good taste in clothes—and the money to buy terrific outfits— but at heart, she's a tabloid girl. I caught her once reading the *Enquirer* or maybe it was the *Globe;* anyhow, she blushed and assured me she didn't believe a thing in it, but—yeah, *but*—she just had to find out what happened to Bob Newhart.

"This must be very tough on you, Barb."

As if she cared.

"I hope they fry that bastard—or inject him, or whatever they do to them these days. Men! Why are they like that? Do you have someone you can talk to? Have you thought about using a professional? Let me give you Bob Wiggy's number. He's that psychiatrist who went in with Spence on that Sherwood Estates thing."

I said nothing, just let her rattle on.

She told me how useful and admirable my life was compared to hers. What crap. What she really believed was that I was a nut-case, a delusional would-be artist, a poor relation.

Okay, I envied her—some of her. I wouldn't have minded having her income (if I didn't have to have her job) and her clothes, and I wouldn't have minded being happily married to someone like my big brother. He wanted us to like each other. She knew this. That was why she was always trying to butter me up.

You see, I knew her before Spence did. We went to the same high school. Same class. Why didn't I like her? Just high school stuff, but I still didn't like her. I remember one time she almost sat down beside me in the lunchroom, but saw a place at the cool girls' table just in time. I'm ashamed of how I felt but she represented everything I hated about high school. Did I mention she also got good grades? She did. After graduation, we went our separate ways. But two years ago she reappeared in my life dating my recently widowed brother. He told me she told him that she divorced the quarterback because he used to beat her up, and he was now in prison for threatening her with an unlicensed pistol.

Given half a chance, I would have advised Spence not to marry her. But it's just as well that I kept my mouth shut. She makes him happy. Anyhow, there was nothing specific I could have said against her. We're just different kinds of people.

"I just want you to know we appreciate what you teachers are doing."

"Thank you, Amanda."

"I just wanted to let you know."

"Okay. And when I find out about Radio, I'll call you. Bye."

That night, I watched the news for a change. The two "anchors" took turns babbling about the President going to China and the new giraffe at the zoo. Finally, they "went live" to Harry at the courthouse. It was closed at that hour, of course, but Harry delivered his spiel standing on its front steps. He said that Wayland had been questioned and released. He had an alibi.

I knew it! I was right! He was innocent. But I was still disturbed about…about something. Just being right about Wayland wasn't enough. I felt like there was something more I had to do. I wasn't sure what it was, but I was sure I had to do it.

Chapter 13

I decided what I had to do was to call Immaculata's mother. "Hello."

"I told you to leave us alone!"

I nearly dropped the phone.

The person at the other end kept telling me what an awful person I was. I finally broke in and said that I was—had been—Immaculata's English teacher.

"Oh, I think you one of those reporter people."

She was, she explained, Immaculata's aunt. Immaculata's mother was asleep because the doctor had given her a pill.

"Tell her I called, will you? And that I'm so sorry about what happened."

She said she would and added that the funeral would be Friday at the Seventh Day Adventist church across from the Green Meadows Mall.

I hung up and just sat there, trying to get used to what I'd just heard. Immaculata Saperstein didn't sound like the name of an Adventist to me. But what did I know? Only that Adventists had Sunday on Saturday.

I told Arnold I was going to the funeral and wouldn't be at school on Friday. He said he was going, too. It was important, he said, for us to show the community that the school cared.

I said I hadn't realized a school could care. He ignored me.

At the funeral, I saw Mrs. Saperstein down on the front row. There was a little girl with her. I didn't even try to talk to her, though. Too many people around her. However, a couple of weeks later, I saw a woman I thought looked like her in Kim Soo's.

"Mrs. Saperstein?"

She didn't deny it. I introduced myself and told her how sorry I was about Immaculata. She nodded but still didn't say anything, which caused me to babble on. I said something about Immaculata being a good student. And at that, she began to talk. She said Immaculata always did her schoolwork, but her little sister, Ruthy—she was a different story.

Normally I'm pretty standoffish. But I couldn't stop trying to imagine Maria Saperstein's life. Where was Mr. Saperstein? What did her family think when she married a Jewish guy? He must have been, right? Did he become an Adventist? What did his family think? Were her parents Catholics? And how did she and her husband come up with a name like Immaculata. It was all so weird.

She told me that her Ruthy was in the fifth grade but still couldn't read very well, and that she wouldn't do her homework unless someone "sat on her." Maria had consulted her preacher about this, and he had sent her to a child psychologist. The psychologist told her she, Maria, was "the enemy."

"Me! Her mother! Me!"

She got very agitated just telling me about it.

"He tell me I should read to her. But when do I have the time? I have a business. And what stories should I read? I don't know stories. What books do I buy?"

I mentioned the library. She didn't know about libraries. The upshot was that I volunteered to tutor Ruthy—to make up for something, I guess.

All I did was volunteer to help a little girl do her homework, but because of that, Kiesha Johnson thought what she thought, which caused Didimo to do what he did, which is the reason I have been sitting up every night for the past week writing this.

Oh, it's not that simple. I know that. What happened was the result of a lot of other things, and it was never inevitable. Even at the last minute Didimo could have had a flat tire or something. Nevertheless, I think my offering to tutor Ruthy was a key moment.

Maria and I made arrangements for Ruthy to come to my house after school twice a week. As it turned out, Ruthy and I got along fine. Soon she was coming by more than twice a week. I gave her a key because she always got there before I did, and, of course, I began going to her mother's beauty shop where Maria gave me free cuts and coloring jobs. And when she had to rush back to Puerto Rico because her mother was ill, she left Ruthy with me for two weeks.

I read to her. I helped her with her homework. But I think the most important thing I did for her was to let her explore the house. For her it was like a secret cave—or a giant attic. She explored it the way I used to explore the local library.

She didn't know what she was looking for, but I did. She was looking for possible futures. There weren't many of them lying around in her mother's apartment. Ruthy knew that in

America she could, theoretically, grow up to "be somebody."
But in her heart of hearts she was sure she was destined for
nobodyhood. And so she had decided not to try. If she didn't
try, she couldn't fail. And if her teachers failed her, she could
tell herself they were stupid because all they knew was stuff
in books that nobody cared about.

Finding a framed photograph of me playing the piano
when I was about her age, she asked, "Is this the piano in the
picture? Can you still play it? Could I try?"

"Sure," I said, and we sat down on the piano bench side
by side. I really didn't expect anything to come of it. But she
kept at it, and she made progress faster than I did when I was
her age. Her fingers seemed to know more than her brain,
which delighted her. Before long she had learned to pick out
the melody of some pop songs I'd never heard of. More im-
portantly, I think, she learned she could learn.

The girls brought flowers and stuffed animals to school
and left them in front of Immaculata's locker, and they taped
notes to the wall, as if Immaculata's ghost were going to come
read them. Naturally, Arnold ordered the janitor to take everything away. A safety hazard. Yes, I was there when he
said it. The janitor said he would but didn't. He was a sensible man, and Arnold never noticed, since he doesn't leave his
office very often. He did, however, ask the Central office to
send a team of "Grief Counselors" to Pershing. (Since when
have we had "teams" of grief counselors standing by waiting
for some grief emergency?) Anyhow, they set up booths in
the gym, and Arnold sent us down there—three classes at a
time—so we could be taught to "manage our grief."

The president of the S.S. (the Student Senate) put a note in the Bulletin asking for ideas for a memorial for Immaculata. Then at some mysterious moment, our institutional grief was over. The janitor took away the signs and the stuffed animals. Bells buzzed; committees met; and I told Priscilla she could start practicing on my classes.

I read her lesson plan but couldn't understand it, so I said to her, "Just tell me what you want to do."

"Well, see, like, my numero uno objective is ... "

Though I still didn't understand, I told her to go ahead. They weren't learning anything from me. Why not let them not learn anything from her for a change?

"I'm going to give them pifs. "

"What?"

"Pifs. That's short for 'epiphanies.' Do you know that word? It's like for when things just 'click.' My ed. psych prof. says it all the time. 'Pif!' he says and snaps his fingers. He's so smart none of us understand him."

She drew circles on the board. Then turned to the class and explained. "These are circles."

The boys went on copying Eddy's math homework; the girls went on talking or brushing their hair. Clarence was drawing on his forearm with a ball-point pen. Pris turned to draw arrows on the board, and while her back was turned, I darted about the room hissing fiercely, "Sit up!" "Be quiet!" and "Stop that!" When she once again faced the class, I was standing against the back wall as if I had never moved.

"Now we'll act it out," she said.

I watched nervously as she divided the class into groups and assigned each group a color—but neither black nor white, I noticed.

"Your color is what you're for."

The kids didn't "get it." Neither did I. Pris encouraged them to speak up for what they believed in—their color. "Have confidence in yourselves. Don't let anyone intimidate you."

Finally Barney stood up and made a speech "for his color." It was a parody of an argument. It reminded me of that playground rhyme that goes, "I come before you to stand behind you to tell you something I know nothing about." After Barney did his thing, the other kids got into it. They waved their arms, pounded on their deskchairs, and filed the room with cries of, "Green! Green! We want green!" and "Red's ahead!" and "Plurple! Purr-ur-URPLE! We are the Uurple people!"

"Isn't it great to see them come alive?"

"Yes, great. Why isn't your friend contributing?"

"Scully? Oh, she had this last year at her other school. She was in an advanced English."

I looked at Scully Trent. She plainly did not belong in this school. Why couldn't I remember to check her file? What was wrong with me? Early Alzheimer's? Maybe I'd had a stroke without knowing it? That happens. I saw a program about it on PBS.

No, I didn't really think I'd had a stroke, but something was wrong with me. I was sure of it.

Chapter 14

I finally remembered to ask my students if any of them knew a boy called "Radio."

Everybody spoke at once.

"Well, tell him to come see me. It's about a job for his band."

The next day after school, a boy wearing a ski mask strode silently into my room.

Behind him came Eddy announcing, "This is him, Miss B. This's Ray. I told him what you said. About the job."

"Ray?"

"That's my name."

"Do you have another name?"

"Radio. Everybody knows that."

"A last name. And, Ray, take that thing off your head. Does Dr. Mossman know you wear that in school?"

"Hi, there. His name is Raymond Macaloon," said a third boy, whom I hadn't seen come in. "AKA—also known as—Radio."

He was small and stocky and was wearing dark glasses and a T-shirt that said "RADIO." "I'm Eugene Count—Count Eugene. He's the man. I'm the manager. Now, what's this here about?"

"I'm waiting, Ray."

For a moment, nothing happened. Then he peeled off his ski mask and leered at me. "Here it is, my beautiful face!"

Singing to himself, he began moon-walking up and down the aisles while I talked to Eugene.

"Hey, how this person heard of me?" called Ray from across the room. Not waiting for an answer, he grabbed two erasers from the chalk rail and smacked them together inches from Eddy's nose, causing him to jerk his head back.

"Blowin' you off, boy!" chanted Radio, smacking the erasers on Eddy's cheeks and also on the top of his head. "Pow, pow, pow!"

Eddy, delighted to be the object of his hero's contempt, tried to shield his face from the blows.

"STOP THAT!" I roared. Then, more quietly, I asked, "What's the name of your band, Ray?"

"The Gang Bangers. You got a problem with that?" But without waiting for an answer, he leaped to shoot an imaginary basketball into an imaginary basket. Catching the imaginary rebound, he shot the imaginary ball to Eddy, and then, ignoring me, he asked Eugene, "Hey, she know my music? Because you tell her I don't do vio-lin-lins."

"It's danceable," Eugene assured me.

Eddy, who had been dribbling the imaginary ball, realized that he'd been forgotten and called, "Hey, Ray, man, can't you just see you doing some do-wop thing?"

Radio plopped himself in a deskchair, crossed his eyes, and stuck out his tongue. Raising his feet, he extended his arms and trembled, as if an electric current were coursing through his body. Eddy and Eugene hooted and made gleeful saliva noises.

I sighed and asked, "Are you in Ray's band, Eddy?"

"No, my mother won't let me."

It was out before he realized what he was saying. Instantly, the other two pounced. "His momma won't let him! His momma won't let him! Momma's little boy!"

"Who say yer good enough for my band, huh? Your momma?"

"His momma! Ha-ha-he-he!"

Eddy grinned, humiliated but glad to be noticed.

As they were leaving, I called him back. "When's your study hall, Eddy?"

"Uh, first of fifth."

"Good, that's my free period. Here's a pass. Come see me tomorrow."

He looked at me apprehensively.

"I want to go over your reading folder."

Chapter 15

I felt sorry for Eddy. Maybe Arnold was right. Maybe my standards were too high. When he showed up during my free period, I got out his reading folder.

"Sit down, Eddy. So the book you're reading outside of class is *The Great Gatsby*."

"Uh, yeah."

"Have you finished it?"

"Uh, well, not quite."

"Okay, let's talk about it. What is its theme?"

"Theme?"

"You know what 'theme' means. We talked about it in class, remember? What's the book about? Adultery? Or the cultural barrenness and false glamor of the Jazz Age?"

"False, yeah. Buncha knock-offs. The jazz scene back then— it was like rock today. Some of those bands—they're just pretendin' like they're famous, like they're U2 or something."

"Me, too?" I repeated, frowning. But he didn't understand what I didn't understand, so I said, "I'm sorry," which was meant to be an invitation to him to explain.

"About what?"

"Never mind. Tell me about Gatsby's relationship to Daisy."

"Well, uh, they were sort of friends," he said cautiously.

"That's good, Eddy—'sort of friends.' But can you develop it a little more?"

"Well, they didn't understand each other," he ventured. But seeing that I wanted to believe him, he grew bolder. "Like did you see that movie on Channel Three Monday night? These two people—the guy, he was a spy, but really he..."

"Let's stick to the book, shall we? Who represents the real moral emptiness of America? The gangster? Or the bored rich girl?"

"Oh, yeah, that girl was really bored. Basically, you know. Yeah. Bored out of her mind. That's why."

'Why what?"

"Well, uh, why she was like that—like she was."

"Yes, well, what about Gatsby's idealism? Would you say it was misplaced?'

"Uh, not necessarily."

"Do you mean that by idealizing this rich but shallow—even vicious girl that he...that he...?"

"Yeah, she was a bitch. Like because she didn't really care about him."

"Are you saying...?"

I paused, ashamed of myself. I was coaching him, wasn't I?—practically giving him the answers? But that wasn't something I wanted to realize, and so I denied it.

He was looking at me curiously. I said, "Are you saying, what Fitzgerald was saying was that we sacrifice ourselves for illusions? How about that billboard, remember? In the first chapter? The big sign that advertised the oculist?"

"Uh, oh, yeah. The sign. Yeah!"

"The eye-glasses—like the eyes of God. They're a symbol. The eyes can't see, but if they could, what would they see? A dump. Remember the dump?"

"A dump? Yeah. Uh-huh. That was sort of symbolical, too, I think."

"That's right! That's right! Now, would you say that what the author is saying is that he thinks the fresh, green promise of America . . . Remember the green light at the end of the dock? And the part about the fresh green breast of the new world at the end? Okay, is his message that we've, well, spoiled things—that we've turned America into a dump?"

"Oh, yeah, really—a dump. Like the way the Chinese dump on us." Overconfident now, he elaborated. "They get into college because they promise to work for the C.I.A."

He saw that he'd made a mistake and fidgeted.

I knew he hadn't read that damn book, but I really, really wanted to believe that he had. So I told myself that he just couldn't talk about it because . . . because . . . well, because he had to express himself in his own language.

"What made you decide to read *Gatsby*, Eddy?"

"Uh, my sister. She said it would be good for me for college."

"I see," I said, countersigning his hall pass.

What I saw was that I was trying to make myself believe the unbelievable. I also saw that he knew I was on to him and was terrified (not too strong a word) for fear that he would never be the person his parents imagined him to be—a person like his big sister, who was "a brain," and was going to Wellesley.

Chapter 16

Last period was over. My students were gone. Pris was gone. In another minute I would have been gone, too. But Kiesha Johnson came slouching into my room saying, "Lavender say you wanna see me."

"Well, she is mistaken."

Another girl came in behind her. "Who are you?" I demanded, wanting desperately to be home and in my bathtub.

"This's Tia. She's my frien'."

They were both big, good looking girls, but Tia was spectacular—good looking and glossy. I'd never had her in class, but I'd noticed her in the halls. She was very noticeable.

"Gotta go," said Tia. "But don't forget."

"I hear you," replied Kiesha, sullenly.

"Glad to have met you, Miss Butler. Have a nice day."

I watched her leave the room. Where had she learned to talk like that? And then, a little ashamed of the way I'd snapped at Kiesha, I motioned for her to sit down. I wanted to say straight out, "Okay, how far along are you? Have you seen a doctor? Is the father in the picture?" But all I actually said was, "So who do you have for English this year, Kiesha?"

"I hadda see Sweet yesterday. He gimmie this test."

"Test? What kind of test?"

"Yeah, it ask do I ever do myself, you know, and how many birth controls I know about. Stuff like that. Why's he wanna know stuff like that?"

"Well, I don't know, Kiesh, but..."

I couldn't finish. Why indeed? I didn't want to think about Sweet's motives. But how could I not? And I knew about that test he'd given her. It was the famous SEAT: the Sex Education and Attitudes Test. He thought he was authorized to give it because he had a certificate from a workshop on transactional analysis—a summer program. He thought that made him a sexpert. Did Windmuller know he was giving girls that test?

Wanting to get back to the immediate problem, I asked, "So have you decided to carry your baby to term?"

"This term? No, the doctor say it'll come in the spring."

"No, I meant...never mind. So you've decided to have the baby?"

"I guess."

"You aren't sure?"

"I wanna, but he keeps yellin' at me."

"Who keeps yelling at you?"

She started to answer but changed her mind. "Miss Butler, I love babies, don't you?"

"Yes, but...Kiesh, you aren't married—you aren't, are you?—okay, and you're awfully young. Have you thought about putting your baby up for adoption?"

"You want to adopt it?"

"Me? I'm too old to adopt a child. Besides, I ... "

"You adopted Immaculata's little sister."

"What? Who's saying that? Why are you crying?"

"I don't know."

I gave her my box of Kleenex. "Listen, Kiesh, having a baby is going to change everything. Are you listening? Do you hear me?"

"Yeah. Change. I hope so."

I could tell we weren't talking about the same thing. "How do you think it will change things? What do you expect?"

"Yeah, respect. That's what it's about. He think he can boss us just because he ... Well, he can't."

"Wait, Kiesha. You've lost me. Who is 'he'? Who is 'us'? What are we talking about?"

"They say I better do the rules, but I say babies are more important than rules."

"What rules, Kiesha? Whose rules?"

We looked at each other. Finally, I let it go. I moved on. I said, "Does your mother know?"

"I just want somebody I can ... You know. You ever love somebody, Miss B.? Like, you know I don't mean like doin' it."

She grimaced and shrugged and said, "I mean like wantin' to do right by somebody."

Neither of us spoke for a moment.

"I don' need no hep!"

Then get the hell out of here, you stupid girl. No, I didn't say that. But I was getting mad—mad at everything. Mad at the stupid education professors who keep telling me I am wicked if I correct students for saying "don' need no hep." Mad at the auto mechanics who don't pay attention to me. Mad at the fact that I was getting older by the minute and seemed fated to end up as an eccentric, lonely spinster, living with her cat.

Leaning forward, I said as earnestly as I could, "Listen, Kiesh, your baby—it's going to need help from you. Lots of help. And that means you are going to need help, too, from somebody. Babies can't talk so they cry, and you have to figure out what their crying means. It will drive you crazy. That's why you need somebody—somebody to help you, somebody you can talk to. It's no time to be alone."

I took back my box of Kleenex that was sitting on her lap, jerked out a tissue, and pressed it first to one eye, then to the other.

Puzzled, she patted my arm. "It's okay. I'm gonna finish school. Really, I am, and then Mamma says I can go to Grandma's. She's downstate. I'll be outta here and he won't know where. And I'll never see him again."

Maybe I should have tried harder to get her to tell me who "he" was. If I'd gotten her to tell me . . . Well, things would have been different, though not necessarily better. Anyhow, she wouldn't have told me. I sat up straighter, determined to bring this conversation to an end. But I didn't want to be rude. I wasn't brought up to be rude. So I was polite and my politeness led to . . . well, to something I didn't expect. Before long we were chatting like old friends about babies, breasts, bottles, folk remedies, and men.

Without much to go on I found myself trying to imagine her life, and it occurred to me that what she was doing—if very awkwardly—was trying out, so to speak, the idea of being respectable. Of having responsibilities. One minute she was a budding matron, the next a giggly little girl—well—not little physically. Teenagers are a lot bigger these days than when I was in school. What she was not was the surly, loud, easily offended teenager I remembered having in class last year.

"What's that book you've got there, Kiesh? Let me see. Do you mind?"

"It's mine. I got it at the drugstore."

It was a romance novel: *Promise at Midnight.* "Do you like books like this, Kiesha?"

"Yeah, I guess. Tia says they're trashy. But what she know? Ever since she beenta New York, she think she some super model or somethin'."

"Tia? Is that the girl who came in with you? She's from New York?'

"No, she went there with, uh, … uh, on a visit."

"Well, listen, Kiesh, … "

And I told her about Doctor Spock. I said, "He writes about babies, about how to take care of them." I wrote out the title for her.

"I'm an English teacher, remember. This is what I do—recommend books. You can probably get it at the library. Not the library here at school—at the public library. There's a branch over on Walnut."

"A branch?"

Chapter 17

"My last day," said Pris, with affected sadness.

"It's gone so fast," I said, playing along.

We embraced.

"You're the best, best master teacher I ever had. I feel like—like—like I've really, really, really made a difference. Don't you think I have? Here's the evaluation sheet you have to fill out on me, and my prof would like a little, you know, paragraph on my personality and all. Okay? Oh, boy, what a day for us, huh?"

We walked downstairs together, and while she was saying goodbye to Shirley's violets, I checked my box and found one of Arnold's "Little Reminders." It was about our restroom duty. Somewhere there is a restroom duty master roster. (Shirley would know.) But we stopped supervising student restrooms years ago. Lyle refers to them as "liberated territory." Sometimes in an emergency a teacher will use one, but it is not something any of us do without trepidation.

I dropped Arnold's "Little Reminder" in the wastebasket and turned around to find Justin Sweet confronting me. He had me with my back against the wall. We stared idiotically at each other.

"Didimo," he finally blurted—and raised his eyebrows. "Your student," he added, giving me another hint.

"What about him?"

He looked around furtively, then leaned closer yet and whispered, "You didn't ever call him the, uh, ahem, the . . . that, uh, you know, the, um, 'n' word, did you?"

I glared at him. But then I remembered, and—I just couldn't help it.—I grinned. "Not exactly," I whispered back, enjoying his expression. "I used 'that word,' but I was comparing it to 'Chink.' Anybody complain about 'Chink'?"

Relieved, he assured me that he'd never doubted that there was an explanation. "But you see, this boy . . . He was roaming the halls, and when Doctor Mossman asked him where he was supposed to be, he said your class, but that he didn't go there anymore because you called him a . . . er, ah, um—that word."

"And you believed him, right?"

"Well, he seems like a . . . "

"A 'nice boy'? Are you crazy? He's a thug! A punk. A . . . "

"Oh, Barbara, Barbara, let's not be judgmental. What we have here is simply a very human misunderstanding. Would you like to talk to him?"

"Shouldn't we *all* talk to him?" burbled Jenny, who had joined us. "I had a course in miscommunication last summer when I refreshed my credentials."

"Would you like that?" Sweet inquired, rapidly clawing his beard. "Yes," he answered himself, "perhaps that would be the way to handle it."

"Transfer him to another class. He hates me."

Speaking in unison, Jenny and Justin assured me that this wasn't—couldn't—be true.

"You are a wonderful teacher."

"You mustn't think of yourself as a failure."

"I'll set up a meeting with him . . . " Justin began.

"In my office," Jenny finished.

"Is that convenient?" he asked, dreamily, clasping his hands before his chest and making a steeple of his index fingers.

"Don't you worry," Jenny cooed, patting my arm.

Then Sweet took off "the roof" and all three of us looked down at the wriggling digital "people."

Chapter 18

The next day Ralph Treadway stopped me as I entered the main office. Scratching his crotch, he informed me I didn't have to worry about Alan Mooney any more.

"Alan Mooney? I don't have a student named Mooney."

"Sure, you do. I've got your memo about him. Well, so I called his parents, and I told them! I said, we can't lock them in 'cause of the fire rules. So he can leave if he wants, but if it's without permission, then we can't be held responsible."

"I've got a meeting, Ralph."

He followed me to the door. "What we need to do, see, is we make a carbon for each pink pass. Wouldn't it be more efficient if we had our pink pass pads made up with carbons between each sheet? How about that, huh? Then we'd have evidence. Our asses would be covered."

"Excuse me, Ralph, I'm late."

"Everything is okay," announced Justin as I entered Jenny's office.

"A misperception," Jenny cooed. "A lack of communication."

"On everybody's part," Justin emphasized, looking from me to Didimo and back with impartial benevolence.

I was uneasy. Didimo didn't look normal—that is to say, like his normally sullen self.

"Because we are all sensitive, intelligent people," said Justin, spreading his arms—an inclusive gesture.

Slumped in his chair, Didimo said he got so discouraged sometimes he felt like walking out of school and never coming back. Jenny and Justin implored him not to do that. When they noticed that I wasn't adding my entreaties to theirs, they silently signaled me to do so. Then Didimo said another reason he wasn't coming to my class was that he felt so bad when I criticized his work.

Justin explained that I hadn't really been criticizing his work. "You weren't, were you?" he asked, shaking his head "no" and nudging me with his elbow.

The phone rang. Jenny answered it. Someone knocked on the door. Justin went to see. While they were busy, Didimo gave me the finger. Jenny hung up. Justin came back. And Didimo reassumed his hurt expression. Justin and Jenny were beaming, certain that Reason and Caring Concern had triumphed.

Didimo said he understood that I had "a really hard job" so he didn't blame me for "making mistakes."

"Now hold on!" I exclaimed.

But Justin and Jenny were ushering Didimo to the door. Only when he was gone did they notice I was angry. They hurried back to me, both of them talking at the same time, slathering me with their assumingness.

"Stop it! Stop it!" I told them what Didimo had done. "I am not having that boy back in my class."

Justin said, "I'm sure you think you saw what you think you saw, but you do see, don't you, that this is what you expected to see? He was probably scratching his chin."

Jenny urged me to be sensitive to Didimo's frustrations.

"Yes," said Justin, "he is our responsibility, and even if he did try to provoke you, there is no reason for us to let ourselves be provoked.

Suddenly I was very, very tired—tired of everything. "What am I supposed to do?" I said weakly, "Take him back and let him write 'Chink' all over the boards?"

"Oh, he explained that," said Jenny. "He didn't do it."

"You were angry," said Justin. "I can understand that. But instead of using your anger, you let it take over."

I stared at him.

"Well, as I understand it, first you blamed everyone indiscriminately without attempting to discover the actual perpetrator. If we go that route—the guilt by association route—ho-ho-he-he—we'll all be guilty!"

He spread his arms again and smiled to show the absurdity of that idea.

Jenny said, "It's Didimo's perception that you blamed him for his laughter about an unrelated incident that took place while your back was turned."

I said, "That boy is bad news."

They both looked at me with silent reproach.

"That sort of language doesn't get us anywhere, does it?" asked Justin.

"'Bad' is a layman's term," explained Jenny.

They nodded to each other.

I was furious. But what could I say that they would be capable of understanding? "How could I make fun of the way he writes?" I snarled. "He hardly ever comes to class, and he's never written anything for me to grade."

Justin smiled compassionately. "What I hear you saying is that he doesn't write like we do. But good writing isn't a scientific fact, is it? Who are we to say that his way isn't better than our way? We have to understand his needs."

Beaming, he looked at Jenny. She beamed back at him, then they both looked at me.

"So I'm supposed to just forget that he gave me the finger?"

"Oh, no," responded Justin. "Forget? No. But we have to deal with his hostility. We can't expect these kids to function in the classroom unless we deal with what's happening in their lives. What we have here is a … " He waited.

I out-waited him. He had to finish his damn sentence himself.

"… a challenge and an opportunity. Oh, it can be tough. We in the public sector don't get the easiest material, but doing something with material like this boy, that's where the art of teaching comes in." He leaned closer to me to bask in the glow of my unvoiced gratitude for his wise counsel and support.

I was stiff, resentful, and confused.

"Something bothering us?" inquired Justin. "Something we need to get out in the open?"

Jenny said, "Barbara, you are one of our most valuable teachers. All your students admire you! By the way, have you talked to Kiesha Johnson yet? I just know you can persuade her to do what's right."

The door burst open and a student assistant shouted, "Dr. Sweet? Dr. Sweet? It's Mr. Kumpf!"

Chapter 19

Justin and Jenny bolted from the room.

I just stood there. Then, still nursing my anger, I walked out into the main office. It was empty. A gym teacher named Donna came in.

"Where is everybody?"

Before I could speak she said, "I bet there are clean towels in the boys' gym," and left.

There was a note in my box from Arnold. He wanted to see me. I crossed the hall to his office and knocked. No answer. I tried the door. It opened. That surprised me. Arnold always kept his office locked when he wasn't there. Then I remembered Bert. Arnold must have run off to see what happened to Bert.

I wondered why he wanted to see me. Should I wait? Then I remembered the article in the *Journal*. That story was ridiculous. Reporters will say anything to get attention.

But… I stepped back to the door and peeked outside. The hall was empty. I shut the door and skipped around behind his desk. I expected it to be locked. Actually I hoped it would be, but, no, not today. My hands were shaking. I stopped and took a deep breath. Then I opened the upper right hand

drawer. Socks, aspirin, paper clips, papers. I moved the box
of Kleenex, and there it was!

Unbelievable! But there it was. It was still hard for me
to believe. My hand snaked forward. I jerked it back. So this
was what he meant by "being prepared"! I was exultant with
indignation. Arnold was insane—a man prepared for real to
meet phantoms! But wait, I told myself. Wasn't there actually a lot of violence in the schools these days? Well, yes, at
that high school out in California. And ... well, but not at
any of the schools I knew about. Except, well—that rape in
the book room. And Immaculata. But Immaculata hadn't
happened at school.

Did broken windows count as violence? Did graffiti count?
Was stealing a teacher's purse violence if nobody was hurt?

And what about my nephew, Scott? Last year at Northeast, he'd been robbed by two girls with knives. This year Spence was sending him to Egremont Country Day.

Now that I thought about it, maybe… Don't be stupid, I interrupted myself. Arnold is a menace even without a gun in his hand. This is a school not a movie set. What if a student broke into his office and found it like I did?

Right there in front of me was the "objective correlative" of everything I thought was wrong with the world—its violence and stupidity, its cartoonish oversimplification of everything. This, I told myself, is wrong! Wrong! Wrong! And as a teacher, was it not my job to right wrongs? To correct mistakes? Holding my breath and using only two fingers, I picked it up and dropped it in my purse. For a second, I stood there panting, then I shut the drawer with my hip and got out of there.

I crossed the hall to the main office. Half the faculty was in there now, all of them talking and milling around. Clara was saying how lucky it was that the girls had stayed after class to finish doing their nails.

"What girls? What happened?" I asked.

"Bert—he could have been laying there until the janitor came."

"Lying where? What happened to him?"

Ralph Treadway grabbed my arm. "Hey," he accused, "it wasn't you sent me that note. It was Pisapus."

"Has anybody seen a manila folder with a green tab?" wailed Shirley. "It's got the amendment forms for the Weekly Health and Safety Report in it."

Windmuller, Mossman, and Sweet came in. The teachers crowded around them, asking about Bert—all but Donna, who wanted Shirley to write down that for the second time this week there were no clean towels in the girls' gym.

"Remain calm," said Dr. Mossman.

"It's a manila folder with a green tab."

"Back to normal, folks," commanded Windmuller. "Mr. Kumph was in good spirits when they took him away."

"To the E.R." added Sweet widening his eyes for emphasis.

"Stress," said someone. And everyone agreed that stress had been "a factor."

"Bert can't relax," declared Ruby.

Rising to Bert's defense, Sweet said, "Oh, yes. He told me that when he gets tense he goes to bed and works problems on his slide rule until he feels better."

For an instant no one spoke. Then the men began har-har-ing, tee-hee-ing, and ho-ho-ing.

Confused, Sweet tried to explain that Bert was afraid that if the boys' calculators ever stopped working that there would be nobody left who knew how to use a slide rule. This caused renewed hilarity. The men began shoving each other as they spoke of Speedy Gonzalez, the farmer's daughter, and the Chinaman in the barrel.

I heard fragments of other conversations, too, conversations about relatives and celebrities who had collapsed and died while mowing the lawn, shoveling snow, or sitting on the toilet.

"Remember the time on General Hospital when… "

Jenny, shook a paper cup containing coins, and shouted, "The flower fund! The flower fund! Bert won't get his plant if we don't catch up on our contributions!"

They all assured each other that Bert would be all right—all except Lyle, who sternly warned us that even if Bert lived, he would have brain damage and could expect to have another stroke or heart attack, whichever it had been, in from three to six months. "That's what the statistics show."

"Oh, no," moaned Jenny.

"Oh, yes," affirmed Lyle, observing her dismay with clinical detachment.

Arnold took me aside. "This isn't the most appropriate time, I know, but we need to consult about… "

"Not now," I murmured, absently, as I put on the coat I'd been carrying.

He blocked my way. "Yes, now, Miss Butler, if you don't mind. We'll just step into my office and… "

"But I do mind," I said, wondering what he'd think when he discovered "it" was gone.

"It's about Miss Wentworth," he bleated, falling into step beside me. "Wait! I have to make a report."

Mossman placed himself in front of me and crossed his arms. "Three forty-five," he barked. "Faculty stays until three-forty-five. It's in the Policy Manual."

I put my face close to his and said, quietly, "Get your ass out of my way."

It took a moment for him to register what he'd just heard. When it did, his mouth opened; his arms unfolded; he stepped back. I stepped forward. He stepped back again. I backed him through the office door and out into the hall, where I turned and headed out the front entrance.

The two administrators came trotting after me.

"Are you sick?" one of them called.

"What's wrong, Miss Butler? What's wrong?"

I pushed open the front door, went down the steps and past the flagpole.

My pursuers stopped at the top of the steps. Arnold

shouted, "This is going on your record, Ms. Butler—your permanent record!"

I walked on, delighted with myself—forgetting all about poor Bert. I was intoxicated by the beauty and the promise of the sunlight flashing on the passing cars and by the pigeons on the sidewalk that took flight as I approached and by the paper cup the wind was tumbling along in front of me. Everything was significant, though I couldn't have said what it all signified. I felt like the star of some musical comedy who had been lifted up by the cast and borne along shoulder high. I couldn't hear what they were singing, but I could feel it, and I was "singing" too, along with them—silently, of course.

What were we singing? Who knows? But it was building, building to some rousing climax. I was so sure there was some immense revelation just ahead of me that I was half a block past my parked car before I realized I'd gone by it.

Chapter 20

The next morning—Saturday—I snapped awake and cowered under the covers. After a moment, hearing nothing, I rolled out of bed, and looked in my purse. It—the gun—was still there. Relieved but still uneasy, I opened the curtains. Snow! Snow everywhere. I relaxed. A new life, I told myself, really was possible.

As I put on my robe, the furnace blooped, the floor squeaked, and the refrigerator downstairs turned itself on. But there were no answering noises—no doors opening and closing, no radio music, no voices calling to each other, no water running through pipes. Of course not. I was the only one there.

If that cute detective were a little older ... Or if I were a little younger. How come men get to sleep with younger women—teenagers, even—but older women can't sleep with younger men?

I sneered at myself for even thinking about Mark that way, But I couldn't help remembering a story in the paper about a teacher out in ... Oregon, was it? She went to prison because she had an affair with one of her students. A fifteen-year-old. (Yuck!) But to be fair, kids are bigger every year.

I've had fifteen year olds who looked like they were 25. Seriously. And the girls! I wasn't as ripe as some of them until I was a senior in college.

Mark was no longer a teenager, but he was probably married. And as I checked myself out in the bathroom mirror, I reflected that I had stopped being 'hot stuff' several years ago.

After breakfast, I took a shower, got dressed, and went to my "studio." My parents were the ones who were dead, but I felt as if they were alive somewhere while I was a ghost, haunting their old house. I thought about how little I'd known about them.

My thoughts drifted to other people I used to know—friends from high school and college whom I never saw or heard from anymore. And what of the actors, singers, authors, painters, and politicians, whose names and photographs I used to see everywhere when I was younger.

"All, all are gone, the old familiar faces," I quoted to myself.

Styles change. Stuff disappears. So do opportunities. Did I wish I'd gone to New York to be a painter like I sort of thought I wanted to once? No, I would never have fit in with that crowd. What difference did it make, anyhow? "Fame if you win it, / comes and goes in a minute." (What's that from?)

I was wallowing in angst, cynicism, remorse, helplessness, and gloom. It's delicious if you have a taste for the stuff. Sometimes I do. But I couldn't keep it up. Each time I remembered what was upstairs in my purse, a cheerful amazement broke through my gloom. Life was so incredible. Anything was possible. That gun up there was mute testimony to the fact that life was real, life was earnest—really, really earnest, which made everything different. Better. It was like a revelation or something.

I ran my fingers over the newly primed canvas that was on my easel. The room was bigger since I'd taken my parents' beds apart and put the headboards, footboards, and mattresses against the wall out in the hallway. The room got great light. I was sure I could paint some good pictures in it.

Next week a moving company was bringing me a couple of decades worth of old paintings I'd been keeping in storage. Christmas presents from me to me.

After lunch I went shopping. It was cold. Everyone on the street was bundled up and looked grim. But when I pushed through the revolving door and entered Emery's Department Store, I was suddenly in another world—a bright, shiny, relentlessly happy world. All the clerks wore Santa hats. From hidden speakers, an endless string of Christmas carols proclaimed joy to the world. I strolled past racks of skirts and blouses and robes. I strolled by tables heaped with sweaters or shirts. I passed glass counters lit from within displaying jewelry, perfumes, or cosmetics. Here and there were mannequins, forever young, wearing clothes forever new, all breathing human passions far above.

She looked right at me but didn't see me and stepped on the escalator in front of me. So I said to her back, "Hi, Amanda."

Twisting half-around, she lighted up: "Barbara! Hi-ee!"

My sister-in-law is perfect. Her teeth are perfect. Her face glowed with perfectly blended cosmetics. And her clothes were perfectly chosen and fitted to a body that was fittingly slim.

"You're coming, aren't you?"

"Sure," I said." I was thinking she meant "coming to dinner with her and Spence on Christmas day."

She read my mind and said, "No, no. To Des's."

We stepped off on the second floor and moved out of the way of the people coming off the escalator behind us. "Des" was Desmond Birdwhistle, her boss. Every year she sent me an invitation to his New Year's Eve party. I never went: first, because I doubted her authority to invite me; second, because I wouldn't know anyone; third, because I was pretty sure I wouldn't like anyone; and, finally, because I knew that if I said I'd go, she'd immediately start telling me what to wear, how to behave, and who I simply *must* meet.

She claimed Des would love to meet me because he was very interested in promoting public education, something I did not believe for a minute.

"Met a friend of yours the other day. Absolutely raved about you."

"Really? Who?"

"Priscilla Wentworth."

"Where in the world did you ..." I began.

But at that moment, a small boy came running down the aisle and crashed into Amanda.

"Hey!" she yelped and tried to push him away. But he had hooked one arm through the strap of her purse and as she tried to pull free, she accidentally whacked him with the briefcase she was holding.

Frightened, he cried out.

And that frightened her!

"Stop!" she bleated, tottering on her high heels.

Twisting free, he ran off. Amanda sighed and reached back to steady herself against the counter, confident that it was there—"confidence" is her middle name—and it *was* there—but a tad farther back than she supposed.

I knelt beside her. "Amanda, are you all right?"

Saleswomen leaned over their counters to see what had happened.

Shoppers stopped to watch.

"Help me up."

I extended my hand, but before she could take it, a man crowded me aside and sank to his knees beside her.

"Are you all right?" he asked, moving his hands around her without quite touching her.

"Hello, Justin," I said from behind him.

"Miss Butler! What are you doing here?"

Once again, I reached down to give Amanda a hand, and once again he pushed me away.

"She mustn't move if she's injured. Are you?"

"Only my dignity."

Sweet grabbed my arm. "You know her? You can explain."

"Explain what?" snapped Amanda, who had gotten up by herself.

"I'm his father," he confessed, cringing.

I had never seen Sweet so rattled, not even the time someone set fire to the wastebasket in the main office.

"It wasn't his fault," he whined. "You have to understand. It's the culture. The advertisements. The sugar. It's in everything! And the threat of extinction. Dozens of species go extinct every day! Do you know that? It's like we're on the Titanic. The earth I mean. Did you see that movie? A child's psyche is too fragile to..."

"Stop," commanded Amanda, who was straightening her clothes. "That boy who attacked me—he's your son?"

"Oh, not 'attacked.' Not 'attacked.' He was just..."

"Amanda, this is Justin Sweet. He's an assistant principal where I teach. Justin, this is Amanda Butler."

"Your sister?"

Amanda looked from him to me and rolled her eyes.

I frowned to keep from laughing. I was afraid he would realize what she thought of him, but, no, he was too rattled to "get" anything. And all at once I knew why. He thought Amanda was a lawyer! It was her briefcase and her tailored suit. I realized something else, too, something I'd actually "known" without knowing I knew it. Justin enjoyed being afraid—that is, he enjoyed imagining he was afraid.

Like Lyle, he claimed to believe the world was going to be destroyed by something or other: Pollution, Sugar, Bigotry, Overpopulation, Corporations, Christianity... take your pick. But unlike Lyle, who expected to observe the apocalypse from a secure position on the couch in the faculty lounge, Sweet liked to think he was teetering on the brink of the abyss. It gave him a rush, but without really upsetting him because at some level he knew he was just pretending. On the other hand, his fear of litigation was real—really real.

Amanda had him figured out in an instant.

"You're afraid I'm going to sue you, aren't you Mr....um?"

"Doctor," he murmured, with a kind of cringing arrogance, and offered her his card.

Looking at it, she said, "Relax, Doc, I'm not going to sue."

"Of course not. Of course not." And made giddy by relief, he stepped forward, saying, "Here, let me help you with that," and began brushing her clothes as if she were a child.

She squeaked and grabbed his hand.

Taking this as an invitation to further intimacy, he put his other hand on top of hers and, with a sensitive, anguished expression on his face, he gazed at her. "Christmas," he said. "A buying frenzy. They want us to go crazy. That's the whole point."

Amanda appealed silently and sardonically to me to do something.

"Is this what we're here for?" he demanded, solemnly.

Before either of us could answer, he bent his knees, peered between us, and waved to someone behind us. We turned to see. It was the child. He was signaling for his father to start chasing him again, to resume their game.

Sweet made incomprehensible hand signals to him. Then, straightening up, he addressed himself to Amanda's breasts: "What do we really want?"

Amused, she pretended to think.

"A new religion," he revealed, looking up at her with bug-eyed sincerity.

"A new religion," she echoed, smiling, having correctly judged that, having no sense of humor, he would be unable to tell she was mocking him.

He told us he was in the process of developing a new religion. It would combine the best of modern science, Zen, and Maslow's theory of self-actualization.

"Do you know Maslow?"

Amanda was laughing openly now.

Noticing this, he started laughing, too, as if they were sharing a joke, and for the first time it occurred to me that I might learn to like Amanda.

She read aloud from the card he'd given her: "Justin M. Sweet, M.A., Ed.D." Then leaning close to me, she muttered,

"What does this mean?"

"Assistant principal," I muttered back. "He 'coordinates with the community.'" I was going to explain this meant he ordered supplies, and worked with the companies that ran the cafeteria and the school buses. But before I could do this, Justin raised his hands, made "V" signs with his fingers, and chanted, "Simplify, simplify, simplify."

"What's he doing?" asked Amanda, nudging me.

"Imitating an insect?" I suggested.

"Quotation marks," he explained, with a look of tender, indulgent superiority. "I was quoting Thoreau."

Lowering his arms, he waved at the shoppers and asked, "What do they really, really want?"

"A new religion," we chorused and were wrong again.

"A real community," he corrected us.

Leaning forward, he confided, "Tomatoes—they don't taste like tomatoes anymore. Have you noticed that? Nothing's real anymore."

"Tomatoes," I echoed, wondering about the reality of this whole encounter.

Amanda was looking at him strangely. I couldn't imagine why. I mean, he certainly is strange, but it was as if she were considering a purchase. I half expected her to ask him to turn around so she could see him from all sides. And he was looking at her as if he were hypnotized. It reminded me of one of those PBS nature films where the mesmerizing snake is about to strike the mesmerized rabbit.

Pressing his palms together with his fingers spread and his thumbs hooked under his chin, Sweet bowed his head and looked up at her from under his eyebrows: "Forgive me. I'm not usually so …"

His pious expression changed to a scowl. "PUT THAT BACK!" he roared and charged between us like a berserk linebacker. Grabbing the pink plastic gun his son was holding, he tried to jerk it away, but the boy hung on to it, making it go klickety-klack, klickety-klack as they struggled.

Amanda touched my arm, "I've got to go," she said, and then she smiled and winked. "Coordinates with the community, right?"

The words obviously meant something more significant to her than they did to me.

Before I could ask what she meant, she reminded me, "New Year's! Don't forget." And waving to Sweet, she called, "Nice to meet you, Doctor," and was already past Purses, Handbags, and Scarves before he could reply.

"Merry Christmas, Justin," I called, as I, too, hurried off.

"Happy Holidays," he shouted, louder than necessary.

He was correcting me, reminding me I had lapsed into "Oldspeak."

Chapter 21

Christmas day I dutifully presented myself at my brother's house.

"B.B.'s here!" he trumpeted, as if a crowd were waiting for the news.

"Your aunt's here," Amanda called to her seventeen-year-old stepson, Scott.

I saw him through two doorways. He was lying on the rug in the den, watching TV.

Six years ago, Nora, his mother—the girl Spence married right after college—was killed by a drunk driver. Scott and Spence both fell apart. Spence would show up at his office looking like he'd slept in the park. Scott started skipping school with a girl who looked like a raccoon.

I moved in with them and did the sister thing. But I certainly didn't want to do it forever. So I was glad when Spence told me about a woman he'd met named Mandy, never suspecting it was Amanda. Nor did she realize Spence was my brother.

When Spence introduced us, there was a split second of mutual shock, then we both started acting like we'd been dear friends in high school. I'm sure Spence believes this. It's what he wants to believe.

After Amanda divorced her drunken quarterback (the coolest guy in high school), she got a job in the typing pool of a local bank. One of the VPs picked her to be his secretary. When a bigger bank bought her little bank, her boss moved up and took her along. When that bank was "absorbed" by C.T. Denbow, he moved up again and once again he took her along. But when he was fired, she didn't go along with him. Instead she became a special assistant to Desmond Birdwhistle, the CEO of C.T.D. Actually this didn't surprise me. Amanda always struck me as the kind of girl who was counting cards in her cradle. However, Miss Perfect did surprise me one afternoon when she confided that she had a secret tattoo. She just never seemed like the tattoo type to me. But she pulled her skirt up and her panties down and there it was. It says, "Born to lose" in curly cursive script.

That message surprised me, too. Nobody wants to win more than Amanda.

She wants Tanya, her daughter, to be a winner, too. Tanya was two years old when her parents divorced. Amanda got full custody, and Spence is in the process of adopting her. He buys her dolls and frilly dresses. Amanda buys her games that are supposed to raise her IQ or improve her SAT scores.

For a while she tried to make Scott a winner, too, but when he made it clear he wasn't going to cooperate, Spence made her back off.

When she learned I was a painter, she wanted to introduce me to "the right people."

"You're marketable, Barbara. Do you realize that?"

Yeah, sure I am.

She particularly likes the paintings I did of Spence's dogs.

"Pets are a niche market. People are insane about their pets. You could clean up."

"'I have a horror of success.'"

"Huh?"

"It's something Van Gogh said—in a letter."

"Wow, Van Gogh ... But, hey, in five years, who knows? With the proper handling and promotion ..."

Looking back, I think she thought my indifference to "success"—to her idea of it—was my way of being critical of her—of her passionate desire to be the best at everything she did, and she had been—almost. That first marriage of hers ... I didn't know the whole story, but obviously it had not been success.

Once in a while, though, I got a hint that there was more to her than I knew about. Like when I was looking at one of the paintings I'd given Spence. He'd hung it in his dining room. Every time I went over to his house, I looked at it because something about it wasn't right. Amanda came up behind me and asked what I was doing. I told her I'd decided to repaint part of it.

She grabbed my arm and with totally inappropriate intensity said, "Barb, we've got to move on. We can't get bogged down trying to do over the past."

Then a timer dinged in the kitchen and she rushed off. I still haven't retouched that picture.

Scott rolled over. "Hiya, Aunty Barb."

Amanda grabbed his upraised hand, hoisted him to his feet, and bustled him into the living room, where she sat him down beside Tanya in front of the Christmas tree and gave them both presents to open.

"But not yet. Wait for the signal." Backing away, she aimed her camera. "Ready, Spence?"

"Ready," he replied, aiming his own camera.

"Okay, kids, blast off!"

Tanya tore into her present with proper enthusiasm. But Scott opened his with provocative slowness and had to be given another one and told to smile this time.

Amanda and I carried platters and bowls from the kitchen to the dining room table. Our conversation, as we passed and re-passed each other, was as showy and unnatural as the narcissus my mother used to force in the middle of the winter. When she asked me if I thought "Mr. Turkey" was done, I winced, and, not for the first time, reflected that she reminded me of my mother.

At last Amanda surveyed what she had wrought, and it was good. She moved a plate or two a fraction of an inch, and it was even better. "Perfect," she said and yoo-hooed for the men. She put them in their places, too.

"Okay, let's start."

There was no blessing. That was a difference from Christmas dinners at my parents' table. But the table-talk was much the same. It ranged from the price of frozen orange juice to the merits of various restaurants and television shows, avoiding anything too contentious or too inappropriately enjoyable, like the stupidity of pretentious actors and the cupidity of pretentious politicians.

"How on earth did you meet Priscilla Wentworth?" I asked Amanda, as I passed the three bean salad on to Scott.

But Spence, sounding very much like our father, cut off her reply by telling Scott to straighten up and get his face out of his plate. Spence's easygoing charm seems to curdle when he is dealing with his son.

To prevent the lecture on manners I sensed was coming, I asked Scott, "How do you like Egremont Country Day?"

Amanda, unaware that for years I had urged Spence to send Scott to a private school presumed that since I was a public school teacher I was going to criticize Egremont.

"Actually there's more real diversity there than at his public school."

"Diversity?" I was flustered. How did "diversity" get into this conversation? But I didn't ask. "Diversity" is becoming a fashionable word and Amanda is fashionable. So I ignored "diversity" and asked Scott if he'd started sending out college applications.

"I keep telling him to aim high," said Amanda.

"He wants to go where he can major in snowboarding," snapped Spence. "Or parasailing," he added. "Anything that gets him going fast enough to break his neck."

"It's Christmas. It's Christmas," tittered Amanda, nervously. And then just between us, she told me I had dark circles.

"Have you been getting enough sleep? I've got some pills..."

Inwardly, I shrank from her concern, but it must have showed outwardly, too, because Spence asked, "What's the matter, Sis? It's Christmas."

After dinner, we "adjourned" to the den where we sat, listless and glassy-eyed, letting the people on television do our living for us.

Spence's stomach growled. "Excuse you," he said, patting his stomach. Amanda leafed through a copy of *Forbes.*

Only Tanya was missing. She was in her room having fun, according to her mother, with the educational games she got for Christmas.

Scott was lying on the rug, watching television. When his boredom grew acute, he rolled himself violently back and forth for a moment and then lay still again.

I reminded Amanda that she'd mentioned meeting Priscilla Wentworth. "When did this happen?"

"Oh, she was with Betsy Pagilia and her daughter. Betsy's in town over Christmas and came by to check in with Des. He's one of her big supporters."

"Betsy who?" And then it came to me: "Our representative, right?"

Amanda looked at me like I was a half-wit. "She's a big friend of public school teachers."

"Not of this one. I never met her."

"Oh, Barb, of your union. It's her biggest backer.'"

"You say her daughter was with her? Is her name Scully?"

"Yes, but why?"

"I've been told I have our representative's daughter in my class, but the Scully I've got in class isn't Scully Pagilia. She's Scully Trent."

"Wow! That's so cute."

"What's cute about it?"

"Well, Betsy was in a pretty tight race last November, remember?"

"So?" I said.

"Well, so Bets took Scully out of her school in D.C. and enrolled her in a local school."

I must have still look puzzled.

"It was to keep her opponent from calling her a hypocrite. The kid won't be back in your class this coming semester. Bet on it."

"Could I have a horse for my birthday?" asked Tanya, entering the room.

"No, you may not."

"Scott gets to go to the Caribbean on his spring break."

"It's a field trip. Tropical ecology. Two of my teachers are taking us."

"If you get caught bringing back marijuana, don't bother to call," said Spence.

Scott snickered.

Ignoring them, Amanda said, "We've been delighted with Egremont. Scott simply wasn't learning at his other school."

"The public schools are a lot worse than people think," I said.

Then my brother and Amanda both began defending the public schools. This has happened to me before. People tell me how bad the schools are, but when I agree, they get upset.

"You do tend to exaggerate, Barb," Amanda insisted.

"Betsy was married before, huh? I mean, since her daughter's name is Trent."

"Oh, yeah. To Taylor Trent. He works for us now—for Denbow. He's a lobbyist."

"Hey, Sis," boomed Spence, "are you still retiring this year? Have you decided what you're going to do with yourself?"

"Nothing."

Scott gave me a look. He liked that.

Spence didn't. He said, "It's a chance for a fresh start, Sis. A chance for you to do something with your talent."

"Would that make you feel better about my wasted life?" I said it smiling, but he knew I was angry and assumed I was angry with him, which I sort of was, but really I was angry at myself. Why? For wasting my life, I guess.

"Why'ncha paint some nudes?" asked Scott, leering.

"Do you still want to be a lawyer?" I asked him.

"Be a doctor," ordered Amanda. "Lawyers are a dime a dozen these days."

Scott rolled over, spread his arms, and stared at the ceiling, like an explorer who'd been captured by headhunters and was staked to the floor of the jungle.

"Don't be a teacher," I said and was taken aback by his braying laughter.

"Maybe I'll write a novel about my sexual adventures."

A sensation! Spence gaped. Scott grinned. Amanda asked me if I'd ever done any writing before. She urged me to go to a writer's workshop.

"Lots of famous writers teach at those things. You could make some contacts."

"Or maybe I'll sell cosmetics."

Everyone grinned and relaxed.

"By golly, you had me believing you," roared Spence.

"Excuse me," I said as I stood up and left the room.

Taking refuge in the master bedroom, I sat on the bed and gazed idly at the bookcase. A whole shelf was devoted to Amanda's astrology books. Did she really believe that stuff? I looked at the shotguns in the gun cabinet. Why did Spence need three of them?

Spence and Amanda were good people, I told myself. Dependable people, the kind of people who made the world

work. And what kind of person was I? A fraud, who posed
as a teacher but did not, in fact, teach. An aging spinster. A
nut case, who was currently infatuated with the idea of being dangerous. I took Arnold's gun from my purse, just to
look at it, but hearing someone coming, I stuffed it under a
pillow and composed myself.

"Are you mad about something, B.B.?" asked Spence as
he sat down beside me.

He was between me and the pillow!

Rubbing my knees to conceal my trembling, I said, "No,
just tired. Christmas, you know."

"Amanda thinks you could teach at Egremont. Why don't
you apply? It would be a lot easier. Better material."

"They'll be wondering," I said, standing up.

He pulled me back down. "Wait, I've been meaning to
ask you. When do you think we can turn the folks' old barn
into cash?"

I didn't say anything. I knew that the sensible thing to
do was to sell it. The house was too big for me. On the other
hand it was nice having all those walls for my pictures.

He said, "I've heard that they're going to widen
Seventy-Fourth Street and link it to the interstate. When that
happens, property values in that neighborhood are going south."

"I'm thinking," I said, "of buying a gun."

"Wow, Sis! You keep surprising me. But that's smart. Our
old neighborhood just isn't what it was. What kind are you
thinking of getting?"

"What kind should I get?"

He was all business, sober, prudent, knowledgeable.

"You'll need to take a course before you buy one. They
usually last a couple of days. Let me give you a name."

As he wrote on the note pad he kept beside his bed, he
said, "I took Mandy to this place last year. She liked it so

much we joined a gun club. Okay, here. Ask for this guy. They charge you about three hundred bucks, and you'll need another three for ammo."

I was imagining Amanda standing behind one of those counters, wearing those ear muffs, and blasting away with some huge pistol. Did she fantasize that she was some kind of secret agent? Some sort of female avenger? Who did she fantasize she was shooting? The quarterback? The whole thing was ridiculous. I couldn't see myself playing silly gun-games. I had never intended to buy a gun. I just said that to keep from getting into an argument with him about selling the house. Little boys play with guns, not grownups.

The silence went on too long. So I asked, "Will I be strong enough to . . . you know, pull that thing back?"

"To cock it? Oh, sure."

To my surprise, he pulled open the drawer in the table beside his bed and took out a pistol. "Here, try it. Like this, see."

"Momma says it's time for ice-cream," announced Tanya, appearing in the doorway.

We both stood up. He waited for me to walk out first, but I said I had to go to the bathroom, and when he was gone, I snatched my gun from under the pillow and looked around for my purse. It wasn't where I left it! Then, thinking I heard him coming back, I rushed to the closet, and shoved it in the pocket of my overcoat.

Panting, I listened. False alarm. Then I spotted my purse where it had slipped off the bed to the floor. I picked it up and hesitated but decided to leave the gun in my coat. In the living room, I sat down next to Tanya. Amanda offered me a plate of cookies.

As I was hesitating between a lemon crunch and a chocolate chip, I heard her say, "Tanya, you're dripping. Go get a Kleenex."

"Aunt Barb's got some."

"Tanya, get out of your aunt's purse!"

Gently, I removed my purse from the child's hands. "What were you looking for," I said pleasantly, "a gun?"

"Tanya, you don't just open somebody's purse."

"It's not somebody's. It's Aunt Barbara's."

I couldn't believe I'd said what I'd just said. What if "it" had been in there? What if Tanya had found it and announced it to the world?

But it wasn't in there, was it? No, because I had cleverly removed it and put it in my coat. I felt special—chosen! For what? I didn't know, but for something!

"Who wants coffee? I'm taking orders," called Amanda.

"I've got to go," I said.

Amanda was irked. In spite of or because of her screwed up youth, she was very proper, and it wasn't proper for me to leave before the proper time, which would be when I had worn out my welcome and everyone, including me, was wishing I'd gone home an hour earlier. That was the "proper" time.

Before Amanda could urge me to stay, I was returning from the bedroom wearing my coat and saying what a WONDERFUL time I'd had, how GOOD the dinner had been, how I LOVED my presents, and how it just WOULDN'T be Christmas without everyone getting together. I kissed Amanda, kissed Spence, kissed Tanya, and waved to Scott, my secret glee fueling my parody of Christmas cheer. Then suddenly I was outside, alone, walking across the snow-covered yard to my car.

Standing in the open door behind me, my lovely sister-in-law called across the yard, "Don't be a stranger. Take care. Bye-bye."

The streets were nearly deserted, this being Christmas, so I could drive fast and I did, congratulating myself on my early getaway. I didn't have to put up with an afternoon like that. A person of my caliber? Certainly not.

Chapter 22

At eleven o'clock on New Year's Eve, I walked up the steps of the Birdwhistle mansion, invitation in hand. Until the last minute I didn't think I'd go, but Radio would be playing, and I was curious to see how corporate America "interfaced," as they say, with the Gang Bangers. Oh, and curious, too—I admit it—to see this "Des" that Amanda was always talking about.

A woman wearing a white blouse and black skirt took my invitation. A woman dressed just like her took my coat. Not knowing where to go, I just stood there, looking over the room. None of the "fat cats," I noted, were fat. A man who happened to be passing greeted me like a friend, and without asking my name, ushered me over to a group by a fireplace. He found me a chair and seemed to introduce me, but in such a way that I introduced myself. He was very smooth. When I learned, later, that he was Desmond ("Birdy") Birdwhistle, the great one himself, I tried to remember what he looked like but couldn't.

Don't gawk, I told myself, wondering what kind of person I would have been if I'd grown up in a house like this. The whole house was graced by the aura of money, which made all things seem possible.

Music was coming from another room. Real music, not Radio's kind. A man named Pitch was resting one hip on an arm of my chair. He said there was a bowling alley in the basement. The woman next to me told me the woman standing by the fireplace was a producer for NBC and was "touching base"  with Vinny (whoever that was) in order "to take the pulse of the heartland in this, the winter of its discontent."

"Discontent?" I blurted.

She looked at me incredulously. "Iran-Contra," she said though clenched teeth.

"Oh, yes," I said, as if it had slipped my mind.

The people around me were talking about how stupid President Reagan was. He frightened them. He knew nothing about economics.

I had always thought rich people were Republicans. I guess not.

Someone to my right said, "Hey, Carter, what's the poop?"

Someone behind me tapped me on the shoulder.

I twisted around and a smirking, obviously drunk young man advised, "Fly now, pay later."

He belched and strolled away, immensely pleased with himself.

I stood up and excused myself. Nobody noticed. I was looking for

Spence or Amanda—someone to talk to. At the foot of the central staircase, I overheard a man say, "It's not cheating. It's creative management." His friend replied, "If you take it seriously, it's a joke."

I found myself chatting with a woman who asked who I was "with." I said, "Nobody, I'm a teacher."

"Oh," she said, "my son is at Egremont. You know, by the time those boys are sophomores, they are doing third-year college work. What college are you with?"

I decided it was stupid of me to have come. But since I was there, I decided to hear Radio's band before I left. I asked a waiter the way to the basement.

"Miss Butler! Miss Butler!"

"Justin! Hello."

His smile was rigid as a pumpkin's—a hairy pumpkin's. Before I could ask what he was doing here, he informed me he was here "on business."

"School business. Educational opportunities. Ms. Cameron, she, uh ..."

"Ah," I said. He didn't notice. Cameron was the quarterback's name. Amanda went on being Cameron after they divorced. But after marrying Spence, she became Amanda Butler on their joint bank account, but at work, she stayed Amanda Cameron.

Sweet was saying, "She wants me to coordinate the Explore-A-Career program. With Mr. Birdwhistle's approval, of course. Do you know about that program?"

I'd heard the men talk about it in the faculty lounge, but had never paid much attention to what they said. Some kind of internship program. But now Sweet was telling me all about it.

"What an experience for them. I'll need time off, of course, but Ms. Cameron says that's not a problem. I'm supposed to meet Mr. Birdwhistle tonight."

I told Justin I was going down the basement to hear the Gang Bangers. He said he would come with me. The Gang Bangers' music got louder. I could hardly hear myself think. Was that the point? To stop people from thinking? It didn't sound like music. It sounded like factory noise. Colored lights swept back and forth across the dancers. They writhed and jerked. But when Radio stepped in front of his band, the dancing stopped. Everybody moved toward Radio. He was up on a temporary stage about a foot high. He was wearing his black ski mask and a leather vest but no shirt. Gold chains glinted on his chest. He paced like a caged animal. He roared. He snarled. I couldn't understand half of it, but it was about dismembering mothers, gang banging cunts, popping faggots, and icing cops. He reminded me of Milton's Satan, bragging of his "unconquerable will" and chanting of "chaos and eternal night." As his drummer batted out a fusillade, he pointed a toy gun at us and flexed his pelvis with astonishing rapidity.

I'd read about "rapping," but I guess I hadn't really believed what I'd read. I was getting a headache.

"He's one of ours," Sweet shouted in my ear. "A Pershing boy. Did you know that?"

I didn't answer. He raised his voice: "That boy—he's from Pershing. He may be a future Pershing hall of fame-er."

I looked at him.

"Oh, I know." He grimaced to show me he, too, disapproved of Radio's lyrics. "But they're all like that today. We have to keep up. And studies show that ... "

"I've got to go," I said. "Goodnight, Justin."

"Shouldn't we stick together?"

He followed me upstairs and continued to follow me as I threaded my way through the crowd who were drinking, laughing, and basking in the glow of mutually certified wealth, intelligence, and beauty.

Someone said, "I'm making a fresh start this year."

"How trite," someone replied.

"No, I mean it. New clothes, new shoes, a whole new me."

Turning a corner, I came up against a woman who turned to me and said, "Doesn't he look like a Legionnaire in that tie?" Then she shrieked, "I thought you were Diane!" and laughed wildly.

Someone said, "Real classics. I saw the price tags."

I felt as out of place there as I did in the faculty lounge. Going up the central staircase, I stepped over the legs of the man who had urged me to fly now and pay later. He was slumped against the balustrades with his eyes closed and his mouth open.

Sweet grabbed my arm. "Where are we going?"

On the step above him, I turned and put my hands on his shoulders. "I am going to find a bathroom. You ... are not going with me."

From the look on his face, I wasn't sure he understood.

"Stay," I commanded. "You. Stay. Here." Then I heard Amanda's voice whooping, "Get ready! Get ready!" And there she was rushing past the foot of the stairs. Raising her champagne glass, she cried, "The end is nigh!" and trotted off to the next room to spread the news.

Sweet went skipping down the stairs after her. And

I, no longer pursued, went back down, too, once again stepping over "Fly now, pay later." Somewhere an orchestra had begun a stately version of "Auld Lang Syne."

People chanted, "Ten, nine, eight, seven…" Whistles tooted. Noisemakers squawked. The band struck up, "Happy Days Are Here Again." People kissed each other. The party took on a new liveliness.

"She got tired of him, that's all."

"They decided their furniture was boring, so they threw it out."

"That guy screws his socks on. He's that crooked."

Spotting Spence, I grabbed his arm and wished him a Happy New Year.

"So you came after all. Have you seen Mandy?"

"She went that-a-way. You know who else I just saw? My assistant principal."

"Oh, yeah. Guy named Sweet, right? Mandy has plans for him."

"Plans?"

"Something about some program Denbow sponsors."

"Explore-A-Career?"

"That's it. The guy who was in charge of it had a heart attack, and Birdwhistle suggested Mandy take it on until Human Resources can find a replacement. But she wants no part of it. She says it's poison."

"Poison?"

"A dead end, I suppose—careerwise. Anyhow, her idea is for Des to hire this guy, Sweet, for the job. A real educator—that's her pitch. Her problem is she wants Des to think it was his idea not hers. Don't ask me why."

I yawned and I told him I was leaving. "Tell Amanda I'm sorry I missed her."

But as I crossed the room, I saw a tiny old lady, a regular gargoyle, on a couch, all by herself. She had on dark glasses and was apparently gazing through them at the yonge fresshe folk who were eddying past her. She looked like she'd been left there a hundred years ago and forgotten.

"Hello," I said, sitting down beside her, "would you like company?"

"Do I know you?"

I bounced back up. So much for trying to be nice.

Extending her hand, she coaxed me back down. "Please. I was napping. You startled me. Who did you say you are?"

"Barbara Butler. I teach English at Pershing High school."

"Pershing? Is that right? Pershing?"

Wow, I'd said something right.

"Do you know Abby? I mean, did you? She taught there. I remember her well. Do you remember her?"

"No, she was before my time, but I know of her. She left some money to be awarded to a student who ..." I could see she wasn't listening. So I asked her to tell me about herself. She perked up and told me she was Desmond's grandmother, Gertrude Birdwistle. Before she married, she had had been Gertrude Emery, of the department store Emerys, and her sister, Mildred, and Abby Coleman had been dear, dear friends.

"My sister collected art. Remember the art shows we used to have at the store?"

I did, though I had totally forgotten them until she mentioned them. When I was in elementary school, Emery's had an art exhibition every spring. They borrowed paintings from museums and local collectors and hung them right there in the store. They couldn't do that today. The insurance companies wouldn't allow it. But things were different back then. Anyhow, my teachers always took us on a field trip to Emery's to see the pictures. I told Gertrude this and mentioned that I was a painter, but it was like talking to a wall. She was too enchanted by her memories to hear anything I had to say.

"The schoolchildren . . . so perfectly behaved. And their teachers—they checked them all for head lice before they came. Remember the silence rooms?"

"Was that what they were called? My mother used to take me to this room in the store where she took off her shoes and rubbed her feet."

"Silence rooms. All gone. Different times. Different people. My father used to say it was the army, the public school, and the department store that . . . "

I never did learn what her father used to say about the army, the public school, and the department store. Too bad. It sounded interesting. But this woman came over and interrupted us. "Lavinia," she said. Her name, I assumed. "Barbara," I replied with equal briskness. The nurse beside her had a name tag on that said "Shirley," but she didn't say anything. Lavinia and Shirley both started telling Gertie, and not for the first time apparently, that it was past her bedtime.

I decided Lavinia–"Vinny"—was Desmond's wife.

Gertie finally agreed to go to bed. But when she stood up, she grabbed my arm, and told Lavinia and Shirley to step aside.

"This young lady will take me upstairs. She knew Abby."

I looked uncertainly at Lavinia for a clue, but she ignored me.

"Grandma, this lady doesn't want to take you upstairs. She doesn't know the way. She can't . . . "

But grandma was having none of it. "Come, dear," she said, tugging my arm.

I resented being drawn into some kind of family quarrel. But Gertie was clinging to me, and I didn't see how I could separate myself from her without letting her fall.

Lavinia ordered the nurse to climb the stairs. Then she squeezed in the tiny elevator with us. Nobody spoke as we were lifted up.

On the third floor, we stepped out into a carpeted hallway. The party seemed a long way off. I don't know what I was expecting, but it was not my abrupt dismissal at the door to the old lady's bedroom, with instructions to leave the elevator in place and take the stairs.

Feeling used and angry, I went down to the second floor and opened a door to a bedroom, hoping to find a bathroom. Instead I found two people squirming and groaning on a bed. Back out in the hall, I considered my options. Music and merriment from one direction; silence from the other. I chose the other and proceeded down a steep, narrow servants' stairs. On the first floor I came to a door with a small round window. I peeked. A bright, modern kitchen packed with bright, modern, young people who were drinking and laughing. I didn't want to go through there—but neither did I want to climb back up to the second floor and go down the front stairs. The servants' stairs went on down another flight. On a whim, I decided to explore.

At the bottom, I pushed through a pair of swinging doors. There was just enough light to bring out the shadowy shapes of old fashioned sinks and stoves. It was, I decided, the original kitchen—the old domain of the Irish girls. From behind the wall came the muffled rumble of bowling balls and the clatter of pins. Then I heard something else. Someone was coming down the stairs! Seized with the conviction that I shouldn't be there, I stooped behind the big table in the center of the room, and then I crawled under it.

Two people pushed through the swinging doors, sending light flashing over the room.

"Where are you taking me?" asked Sweet.

That big rich voice of his sounded like it came from a big manly man.

"Shut up," said Amanda, and threw her glass against the wall, "Nobody comes down here."

"Shouldn't we sweep that up before somebody steps on it?"

She laughed and asked, "What did I just say?"

Backing herself against the table, she scooted up on top of it. Her feet were dangling right in front of my nose.

"Why did you tell them I had to leave?"

"You were embarrassing me is why. Des was beginning wonder why I recommended you. And keep your damn hands to yourself."

"But why did you bring me down here?"

I was wondering that, too.

"It was the quickest way to get you out of sight. If you'd kept talking to those men like you were…Oh, God. I had to get you away before you got me fired."

"You are certainly a strong woman. I admire strong women."

"I can't believe the way you acted with him. You made me look bad."

"Does…Does that mean…"

"Oh, you could still get the job. Des thinks a lot of people are idiots."

This wasn't something I could ever tell Spence about. And not just because it was "a delicate matter." He would be sure to ask, "How do you know?" I would have to say I was hiding under the table, and *that* was just too fantastic. Who could believe it? Would I believe him if our positions were reversed? No, I would think he was crazy—or rather that's what I would have thought. But not anymore. After having actually been in that unbelievable situation myself, I was ready to believe anything was possible.

But how could I face him—or Amanda—or Sweet? How could I keep a straight face knowing what I now knew. But *what,* exactly, did I now know?

Sweet said something about "transcending the whole domination-submission syndrome" and something about "his inner woman responding to her inner man."

Amanda said very soberly, "Sweet, I have never meet anyone remotely like you. You are an utter jerk, do you know that?"

In spite of the way I felt about her, I was glad to hear her say that. I'd wanted to say it often enough myself. Suddenly I was sure I would be discovered. Amanda had been idly swinging her legs with her pumps half off and hooked on her toes. On an upswing one of them sailed off her foot and out into the room.

"Go get my shoe."

"What?"

"My shoe. It fell off."

Petrified, I watched his legs as he scooted off the table and circled the shoe. I was sure when he bent over to pick it up he would see me.

"What's taking so long?"

"I'm being careful of the broken glass."

"Oh, I'll get it," she said, sliding off the table. Bending to pick it up, she looked right at me. and squealed. She jumped back up on the table. but not right above me this time.

"I think I saw..." She giggled and then asserted definitely, "There's someone under this table."

He chuckled his mellow chuckle.

"Now, let's be logical. You think you saw a..."

"Damnit! LOOK UNDER THE TABLE!"

They were drunk. Alcohol is not my thing, so I was slow to catch on.

"Stress," Sweet was saying. "It's stress. What you need to do now is relax. Just relax," he crooned.

"Are you going to look under the table or not?"

"But I've told you. It's not logical."

No answer.

The next thing I knew, he was squatting down and looking right at me. But he immediately bobbed back up.

"Nothing there," he assured her.

I couldn't believe it. Yes, the room was pretty dark, and it was darker under the table, but he had looked right at me. How could he not see me? All I can think is he didn't see me because he "knew" before he looked that nobody was there. It wouldn't be logical for anyone to be there, right? So, ipso dipso, monte crispo, nobody there!

I also decided that Amanda knew she was woozy and must have decided right away that she'd been mistaken, and so from then on, the whole thing had just been an excuse for her to bully Sweet.

"I'm going back upstairs," she declared, raising her knee and slipping her shoe back on. She strode from the room.

"Watch out for the broken glass," he called, hurrying after her.

The swinging doors kept flapping a few times after they were gone, flashing smaller and smaller slices of light across the room.

Chapter 23

I was eager to get home, have a cup of cocoa, and go to bed, but it had begun to snow, so I drove slowly. Then I began to wonder if I had milk in the fridge? I assumed no place would be open where I could get some, not on New Year's morning. But then I saw Kim Soo's red neon sign blinking through windy veils of falling snow. Kim's never closes.

Kim, or one of his relatives, was asleep behind the counter.
"Hey, Happy New Year!"
Jerking awake, he said, "Ha! Hoppy you year, you."
"Do you have a restroom?"
"No. No westwoom."
I silently appealed to him.
Wordlessly, he relented, and led me to the rear of the store.
"Bad storm," he said.
"Thank you," I said. He was nice. I was nice. There was still hope for the country.

Stepping back into the store, I froze and closed the door quietly. Something was different.

Then a lot of things happened all at once. I've tried to sort them out, but I can't. I have no idea what came first, second, or third. I don't even remember hearing the shot. All of a sudden I was flat on the floor. Cans, plastic bottles, and bags of chips had fallen down around me, and my heart was trying to smash its way out of my chest.

Then nothing. Stillness. Silence—except for my heart, which was making enormous thumps as it tried to escape.

Someone moaned.

I shrank into myself.

More moaning. A door opened. I felt the wind. Then it shut.

I don't know how long I lay there, listening, but I finally got up and started creeping down the aisle. When I remembered my gun, I stopped, took a deep breath, and opened my purse. It wasn't there. Of course not. My purse wasn't heavy enough for it to be in there. I'd left it at home. What would I do with a gun at Desmond Birdwhistle's party? I was relieved. But at the same time I wished I had it.

The first thing I saw when I crept around the corner of the aisle was a gun—a much bigger one than mine. It was on top of the counter. Kim was on the floor behind the counter. While I stared at him, he twitched and moaned again.

I had to call the police. There was one of those mobile phones on the floor beside the clerk. It was as big as a brick and had blood all over it. I'd never used one and in my semi-hysterical state, I couldn't make it work, so I ran back to the little cubbyhole office beside the bathroom and used the regular phone on Kim's desk to call 911. I told them where I was and that a person had been shot. The person I was talking to kept saying, "Hang on." But I grabbed an apron hanging on a coat rack, ran back to the clerk, and pressed it against his wound. I didn't know what else to do.

As the apron turned red, I could feel my body shutting down. I was on the floor, unconscious, when the police arrived.

Chapter 24

I shoved my head under a pillow. The phone went on ringing, Finally I picked it up.

"Yes, Spence. I'm fine. What's wrong?"

"Nothing with me. It's you. What's wrong with you? You don't sound fine. Do you need a lawyer?"

"A what? Why would I need a lawyer?"

"Just in case. A woman who works for me—her husband's a cop. She told me what happened at the deli."

"Uh, okay, but why would I need a lawyer?"

"I don't know. I don't know. I'm coming over. He's going to be okay, by the way."

"Who?"

"The Korean guy. You saved his life. Yes, it was on TV. If you hadn't been there and called the cops, he would have bled to death."

"I'm glad he's okay, but Spence, don't come. I need to sleep."

"Do you need some pills?"

"No, I'm good at sleeping. Come tomorrow."

"You're sure you're okay?"

"Positive. Your little sister's just very tired."

I put the phone down and tried to sort out what happened at the convenience store. The paramedics took Kim away. The police took me to the station. They questioned me then left me sitting by myself. I promptly went to sleep. They woke me up and I talked to some other people. I signed something. Finally, two patrolmen drove me back to the convenience store so I could get my car. But it wouldn't start. I sat in their car and slept. By the time they got it started, it was daylight.

I was still wearing the clothes I'd worn to the party. So I took them off and had a bath. It was almost dark. I'd slept all day, so I put on my pajamas. But I'd just got up, so I made breakfast—toast, and coffee—and took it on a tray into the living room. The coffee table in front of the couch was covered with books and student folders. There was no place to put down the tray, and this suddenly made me furious!

At what? My life? The school? My students? The world? I didn't know, but I was furious. I was glad Kim was going to be all right. But why did he have to be shot? Why did these things have to happen? I was getting scared again. I felt like a version of Typhoid Mary, only I spread violence instead of typhoid. Well, that's what it seemed like. Everywhere I went somebody got shot or raped. I wasn't the kind of person I wanted to be around.

Then all at once I didn't care. I was too tired to care. I stood before my front window—my "picture window"—and looked at my indistinct reflection. You look like your mother, I told myself. Was I turning into my mother? I had a portrait of her I'd painted years ago. Last Sunday I showed it to Vern along with some other paintings. I'd asked him to come see them, and he'd stopped by after church, still in his girl get-up. I told him he himself was a work of art, which is true.

I don't know why I showed him my pictures. He doesn't care about art—except the art of making himself up like a girl. I just felt my pictures needed to be looked at by somebody besides me.

He wanted to know if I'd ever "shown them."

I said I was showing them to him.

"I mean in a gallery. Have you ever had a show?"

"Nobody wants pictures like this."

"How do you know that if you've never shown them?"

"Lean them against a fence and sell them on the street? No thanks."

"But if you never sell them, what's the point?"

"What's the point of teaching school? What's the point of anything?"

"You're crazy, you know that?"

He wasn't the first person to tell me that, but he was the first person to say it with admiration in his voice. We both grinned. It was a nice moment, but so what? What good are nice moments? I could have been killed last night. I could be dead, and Spence would be wondering what to do with all his crazy sister's paintings.

I needed to talk. I thought of phoning Vern. But on second thought that seemed like a stupid idea, just like everything else. I was a con artist. That's the kind of artist I was. Education was a kind of Ponzi scheme that depended on a never ending supply of new suckers. (Nobody would buy our snake oil twice.) When parents complained, we assured them that "the system" was being reformed.

Has anything ever been reformed as often as public education?

I blamed my students for wasting my time. I blamed myself for wasting theirs. And in some crooked and devious way I also blamed myself for what happened to Kim, which reminded me...

Back in the living room. I stood before the window with the gun in both hands like I'd seen people do in movies. I was ready for the bad guys now. I felt serious—grown up. What do people take seriously these days? Sex, art, education, marriage? Hah! Religion? Ha-ha! But bullets...Bullets were still serious business. Was that why so many people wanted to own guns?

I hefted it, pointing it here and there, getting used to the thing. What if I killed myself with it? I wasn't serious. But I was seriously weary of the present shape of my life. I considered quitting my job on Monday instead of waiting until spring. I wasn't serious about that, either.

Pointing the gun at the window, I tracked the shadowy man who was stumbling and slipping as he walked down the snow covered sidewalk across the street. He had no idea I even existed. Nobody, I told myself, knows what's really going on.

Chapter 25

I called Shirley to tell her I was going to stay home for at least a week. But Arnold answered instead of Shirley.

"What about your semester grades?" he asked dully.

"Well, if I'm not back by the time they're due…"

"It doesn't matter."

He sounded exhausted. I pitied him. I was sure he had a license for the thing. I was the lawbreaker, wasn't I? And then I pitied myself and told myself I'd done the right thing. He should never have had that thing at school. He needed to be taught a lesson, and that was my job, was it not?—to teach lessons?

Yes! But just the same, I wished Phil had never said what he'd read in the *Wall Street Journal* and that I'd never been in the faculty lounge to hear him say it. I wished I'd never found myself alone in Arnold's damned office and that he'd never left his damned desk unlocked. Who was I to go around teaching lessons? And what was I going to do with it?

I went to Maria's beauty shop to have my hair cut. She knew what had happened at Kim Soo's. It had been on television. But she didn't know I was the unidentified customer who had called the police. And I didn't tell her.

She said she was worried Ruthy was reading too much for a girl.

"She's so pretty. I hope she doesn't get too serious."

Back at the house, I tried to paint but couldn't. So I turned on the TV. On C-SPAN, I caught an awards show honoring The Outstanding Rookie Teachers of the Year. Fifty young men and women were standing in rows on risers behind the MC, who sounded like a game show host.

I stuck with the Rookie Teacher of the Year Awards Show because I'd never heard of such a thing and couldn't imagine how the Rookies were selected or who did the selecting. I didn't wonder long. There she was. On the back row: my very own Priscilla Wentworth. And I realized the awards were some kind of political deal. Shelly or Scully, or whatever her name was—her mother, my congressional representative—had seen to it that, on her daughter's recommendation, Priscilla was a Rookie of the Year.

The master of ceremonies said that all the Rookies were being given internships at the Department of Education.

Of course. They were the future officers of the Great Bureaucracy.

The next morning, I called Shirley. "Hi, did Arnold tell you what happened? Well, I'm coming in tomorrow after all."

"Oh, Dr. Windmuller will be so relieved. He was afraid we'd have to postpone your grades. But we can still do that, you know. There's a form for it. So don't let him make you come back just to turn in your grades."

"No, it's okay. I'm ready."

Chapter 26

Phil and Lyle applauded when I walked into the main office. Max gave me a thumbs up. Shirley, who was on the phone, waved. And Clara, seizing my arm, chirped, "We wuve 'oo, Barby."

They all knew all about what happened at Kim Soo's. How come? I never found out. My name wasn't in the paper, and I don't think it was ever mentioned on TV. Nevertheless, they knew—indeed, they knew more about what happened than I did.

Vern hugged me and said, "A sight for sore eyes, my dear. I prayed for you. Have you seen our leader yet? No? Well, hang on tight. Lyle says irritable bowel syndrome. But my diagnosis is dementia. Hey, what's wrong with you?"

"Nothing. I'm fine."

"You don't look fine. You look flustered. Nervous. Guilty, maybe. What have you done? I mean beside nearly getting yourself shot?

Before I could reply, Ralph Treadway joined us and accused me of failing to return the film and the projector I'd checked out from the A/V room on Friday.

"This is her first day back, Ralph," said Vern.

"I wasn't here last week."

"Is this your room number or not?" he demanded waving a piece of paper.

I turned away but he went on yapping.

"Is this your room number? Is this your room number?"

Stella, who has a hard time speaking English (although she teaches English), said, "Hah! Guud see you, Basha, Ver' guud."

Sweet blocked my way. "A terrible experience for you. Doesn't it seem like the police are always shooting the wrong person? If they didn't carry guns, the criminals wouldn't, either. There would be no point to it, don't you see?"

"I've got to go tell Windmuller I'm back."

"Do you see what I mean? If you need to talk..."

Slumped behind his desk, Arnold looked up when I entered his office, but then immediately looked back into the open upper right hand drawer of his desk, as if by looking hard enough and long enough, he could make what wasn't there be there.

He must have been gaining weight ever since I took his stupid gun, but over the holidays he'd ballooned. He looked exhausted—disoriented. The back of his tie was longer than its front, and his shirt was buttoned wrong. He disgusted me. Everything disgusted me.

Only in a degenerate society could an imbecile like Arnold get advanced degrees, hold a responsible position, and pass himself off as a normal human being!

I wasn't being fair. I knew it, and so I was disgusted with myself as well. I think I might have confessed and given the stupid gun back to the stupid man in front of me if he hadn't suddenly slammed shut his desk drawer and exclaimed, "They're sick and tired of me? Well, I'm sick and tired of them."

Who was this "they" he was talking about? He couldn't be any sicker of "them" than I was of him. So I drew myself up and made the speech he should have been making to me. I said, "Welcome back, Miss Butler. Are you feeling better? If there's anything I can do, just let me know. It must have been a terrible experience for you."

He gaped and then said, "You aren't making sense Miss Butler. Why aren't you in class? It's nearly time for the bell."

Then he poured water from a plastic bottle into a paper cup and took a pill.

Leaving his office, I bumped into Jenny Lavender, who was on her way in. She changed directions and walked me down the hall inquiring anxiously what I thought.

"About what?"

"About him. You saw him. Isn't it awful? It's because he worries about them so much."

"Them?"

"He's so dedicated. A real we-person."

"A what person?"

"He takes the challenges we face so seriously, but they are eating him up, don't you think?"

I walked faster. The hall was nearly empty.

"Those old me-people just go around me-me-me-ing all the time. It must be nice for them. Well, I don't mean 'nice.' You know what I mean. If there were fewer me-people and more we-people, we'd all be a lot better off, wouldn't we? Oh, my, we're walking so fast! What I'm trying to say is—is don't we wish we could do something for him? You know, give him a boost."

"A boost?"

"Eddy Clambering," said Jenny, nearly trotting to keep up.

I stopped and frowned at her.

"I'm sure I can get him into a really top school if he makes an 'A' from you. Wouldn't that be wonderful? Dr. Windmuller would be so proud. We could all be proud. And then everything would be worthwhile."

Waiting for a response, Jenny milked the handkerchief she was holding under her chin.

I said nothing.

Bouncing a little, she added, "Eddy says he asked you if he could turn in extra but you said no. He says you said he simply wasn't an 'A' student. What a terrible thing to say."

"Jen, listen to me. Eddy is not getting an 'A' from me. He doesn't read, and he writes like a fourth grader."

"Oh, but he reads. He does. I checked his scores. He's above grade level on the RSCT. Come to my office. I'll show you his scores."

I glared at her.

"But you gave an 'A' to Nan Wang last semester, and she never made more than a 'C' before."

I just looked at her.

"But you see, since Eddy's always made 'A's,' it will look suspicious, won't it? I mean, it's like you favored Asians."

I started walking as fast as I could.

"Oh, Miss Butler," puffed Jen, trying to keep up. "If there's a conflict—a personality issue—I could transfer him."

"Do it."

"Well, Dr. Windmuller told me you said he was a freak, so I assumed there might be a problem."

Confused, I stopped. "Arnold said what?" Then I remembered. "Oh, I said he was a computer freak. Well, he is. What's wrong with that?"

"But don't you see?"

"Jenny, 'computer freak' is just an expression."

"Oh, Miss Butler, they're all just expressions."

I put both hands to my temples. I had no idea what to say because I had no idea how anything I said would be understood.

"I didn't say it to him, Jenny. I said it to Arnold."

"Still, you said it."

"Transfer him, if you want. I'm not giving him an 'A.'"

I walked on.

Behind me, she called, "I hope-a, hope-a, hope you'll change your mind, Miss Butler. I've got my fingers crossed. See!"

I was at my desk when the bell rang and got right to business.

"Open your books. Page eighty-seven."

They groaned. They said the substitute hadn't made them read anything.

"She just showed movies."

They pointed to the projector on a cart at the back of the room.

"It's poems," reported Barney, looking glumly at page eighty-seven.

I told them I didn't care what the substitute had done. I said it was important for them to learn about Emily Dickinson.

"Why?"

Ignoring Darlene's question, I called out, "Sit up, Eddy. What's wrong with you?"

Clarence blurted out that he was sick of school and grabbed Darlene's pencil. She grabbed it back and said she was sick of him.

He said, "Watcher mouth, bitch."

Genesis said if girls were bitches, all the boys were dogs, and half the boys in the room started barking.

I slammed a book on my desk. Everyone shut up and looked at me.

"We're going to see a film," I announced firmly.

"'Snot 'bout po'ms, 'sit?"

I didn't reply. I was busy closing the blinds. There was a reel already on the projector, and I was going to run whatever was on it. I clicked on the machine and discovered that my substitute had switched the reels without rewinding the film. It was running backwards. I clicked it off.

"Hey, no. Leave us see it like it is."

A chorus of agreement.

"QUIET!"

They were. But there was expectation in the air. They were bargaining with me.

"Pity peese wit sugar on it?" cooed Carmen.

I clicked the machine back on.

It was a documentary about World War Two. To my students' fascinated satisfaction, the narrator delivered all his sentences backward as biplanes landed backwards, bombs floated upward back into bomb bays, and demolished buildings reassembled themselves.

What would I say if Arnold walked in? Well, I would tell him that this learning module was challenging my students' visual prejudices! Yes, and I'd say I was liberating my students from the visual stereotypes of their culture. I'd say I was facilitating a metatransitional sequence to a developmental learning phase that was preparatory to the effectualization of a new plateau of visual literacy.

As I dozed off, I remember thinking, "You aren't making sense," but I told myself, "We all have a right to our own language."

I couldn't have slept long. When I woke, the movie was still going on—backwards—and the dimly visible clock high on the wall above the portable movie screen showed ten minutes left in the period. If I left now and went to the girls' on four, I could be back before the bell. Theoretically, the restroom would be empty. Did I dare leave my class unsupervised?

They would behave, wouldn't they? That was part of the unspoken bargain they'd struck with me, wasn't it? I took my purse from the bottom drawer of my desk and whispered to Carmen that I'd be right back.

"If the film ends while I'm gone, you switch it off, okay?

She didn't respond.

I touched her shoulder. "Okay?"

Half-waking from her trance, she nodded.

Chapter 27

Walking into the girls' on four, I saw Kiesha's friend, Tia, the African-American Aphrodite. She was standing at the washbasins, looking at herself in the mirror. When she saw my image appear in the mirror, she flinched but recovered and went right on refreshing her lipstick. She kept watching me though. I could tell.

At the other end of the room, two girls were sharing a cigarette, and Appaloosa was counting bills into the hand of a girl I didn't know. Seeing me, she practically leaped into a stall and shut the door.

I wheeled around, walked out, and hurried down to the girls' on three, hoping it would be empty. I didn't want to know what Appaloosa was buying or what those other two girls were smoking. I told myself they were probably sharing a cigarette made of tobacco. Of course, that was against the rules, too, unless you were a senior with privileges and were doing it in the senior lounge. But who really cared? Who cared what happened to them after they graduated? All anybody cared about was covering their ass.

Take Bert and that mess he got into last spring. He was leaving school well after the last bell and came upon a boy who was pissing in the empty hall. Grabbing the boy's arm, Bert demanded his name. The boy knocked him down, zipped up, and walked off.

Bert wrote a note about the "incident" and sent it to Arnold. So Arnold put a note in Bert's file reprimanding him for unprofessional conduct. Touching a student is unprofessional. Max vowed to make a union issue of the reprimand. Arnold said he had no choice since Bert had "put it in writing." Bert pointed out that the pisser hadn't complained. Finally, Arnold offered to remove the reprimand from Bert's permanent file if Bert would remove his written complaint. At least that's what I heard happened.

Didimo came around the corner at the far end of the hall. Seeing me, he hesitated but then came on towards me.

"Hi, hon," he said, as we passed.

He was breathing heavily, and, yes, it did occur to me to ask him where he'd been during my first period that morning (and many other mornings), but I didn't. I had a more pressing issue on my mind.

Preoccupied with myself, I turned the corner, and then I stopped.

The door to the boy's john was half open. I could see a man's legs. Someone was lying on the floor.

"My head," groaned Vern, as I knelt beside him.

"I'm going for help," I said and dashed into the nearest classroom, intending to call the office on the intercom, but what I saw made me forget what I had come to do. Max Tinder was standing on top of his desk, addressing his class.

Recovering from my astonishment, I pressed the intercom button on the wall and shouted into the speaker, "Shirley! Shirley!"

"What's going on?" shouted Max, getting down from his desk.

"Shirley? Shirley?" I called.

"It's broken."

Having already figured this out, I was on my way out of the room when Max grabbed my arm, repeating, "Wait! What's going on?"

His class followed us into the hall.

"Get back!" I ordered, placing myself astride Vern.

But then the bell buzzed, and all up and down the hall classroom doors opened, and shouting, jostling students poured out into the hall. The crowd in front of the john grew larger.

"I gotta go!" said a boy, trying to shove me aside.

I grabbed his arm, "Go to the office and tell them that..."

He jerked free. "I gotta go now! You wants me t' pee ona floor?"

Seeing Eddy, I called to him, but he pretended not to hear and slunk away. Then, seeing Kiesha at the back of the growing crowds, I called to her. "Go downstairs and tell them Mr. Harmon has fallen down. He's hurt. He hit his head." She squinted, indicating she hadn't heard what I said. I was surprised she was still coming to school when she was so far along, but there was no time to think about that just then.

I pulled her close and, talking under the noise, repeated my instruction. This time she nodded and hurried off. Meanwhile, Max had dragged Vern inside the john.

"What'd you hit me for like that?" screeched the boy who had tried to push past me. "You got no right to hit us!"

"Yeah," another boy chimed in. "We got rights!"

"Hey, Miss B.," called a genial basketball player, "Don't let 'em give you a hard time."

"Our rights to bodily functions. It's in the Constitution!" said other boy.

When I glared at him, he grinned.

"What's going on?" called a newcomer.

Raising both my arms, I told them Mr. Harmon was ill and urged them to go on to their next classes. I said that the office had been notified.

"Hey, I can give CPR. I saw it on TV."

The second bell buzzed, and they dispersed. They were already late to their classes, but it wouldn't matter; they had a story to tell. I stepped inside the john. Max had Vern sitting against the wall. His face was bruised and swollen. His toupee was on the floor. (I had always suspected he wore a toupee, but it was still a shock to see his bald head.) He was more alert now. I watched as he removed a loose tooth, and licked back a dribble of blood.

"I was headed to the lounge," he whispered, "but then I thought…Ow! Stop. It's my knee. I thought why not just use the boys'. But there was this girl…"

"A girl!" exclaimed Max. "That's against the rules! What was she doin' in there?"

Vern grimaced and grinned at the same time. "She was being rogered."

"Roger? Roger who?"

"She was being had."

"Had? Had? You mean…You tryin' t' say she was being fucked?"

"Are you sure you can stand?" I asked as Vern, with Max's help, levered himself to his feet.

"You won't sue us, will you—if your ankle's broken?" asked Max.

"Why should he sue us?" I asked.

"Why should I sue you?" echoed Vern.

"Because this state doesn't have a Good Samaritan law. So if your ankle's busted and we make it worse by helping you walk, you could say you were too confused to know what you were doing and..."

"That's crazy," I said. "I never heard of that law."

"That's because we don't have it."

"Oh, stop," exclaimed Vern as he gingerly put some weight on his left leg.

I held the door open.

Max grasped Vern's left arm.

Vern took a tentative step forward.

Windmuller and Sweet came around the corner at the far end of the hall and hurried towards us.

"Oh, thank God," exclaimed Windmuller. "Thank God, he's alive."

"This girl—she said you were dead," explained Sweet motioning towards Kiesh, who was standing behind him.

"What happened was these guys beat the crap out of him because he tried to break up a gang bang," explained Max.

We all looked at him.

"Yeah, they dragged her into the john and were raping her when Vern walked in. So then they attacked him. Lemme tell you, the union's gonna have something big to say about this."

"One girl. One boy," Vern murmured. "And she didn't seem distressed."

"How can we teach without protection?"

"They had no protection?" asked Sweet, with an anguished expression.

"What I'm saying is, hey, do we get some real cops around here or not?"

Sweet asked Vern, "Why did they feel they had to resort to violence? What did you do, do you think, to provoke them?"

Arnold noticed Kiesha and rounded on her demanding, "Why aren't you in class, young lady?"

She flared back. "Don't I 'posed t' have a pink pass?" But then she looked at me, held up a worn paperback: *Baby and Child Care.* Smiling shyly, she said, "Pretty tough, Miss Butler, but I'm readin' it."

We both smiled. I told her to go to my room and wait.

"I don't suppose you know who, uh ..." suggested Sweet, as he grasped Vern's right arm.

"No, I don't," Vern replied, grimacing as he hobbled between Sweet and Max.

I gave him a look saying I knew—and that I knew he knew I knew. He gave me a look back that said, "Just shut up!"

"Probably outsiders," said Arnold. "Oh, yes. In spite of all our security, they get in here and what can we do? They look like perfectly normal students."

Max declared, "Rapists ought to go to hell for life."

Sweet was appalled, but he smiled diplomatically and began explaining that rape was an entirely understandable Darwinian response to the threat of species extinction. "Its root cause is ...? What?" He looked around to see if any of us knew the answer. "Stress," he replied. "Anxiety about the destruction of the environment triggers a reproductive imperative."

Pleased by the sound of this, he straightened his back and raised his chin which caused him to tilt Vern toward Max.

Vern gasped.

Max, feeling obscurely challenged, tilted Vern back towards Sweet.

Vern gasped again.

A few steps ahead of us, Arnold was muttering about "remediations" and "multifaceted interactions."

Only his thighs replied, making a dismal, rhythmic hissing as he walked.

"What?" I asked, thinking he'd spoken to me.

"Systemization," he muttered. "Lifestyle facilitation. Needs assessment inventories. If we only had the money to do follow-throughs on self-actualization agendas..."

Once upon a time I had actually—well, sort of, almost—believed that crap. I was young and didn't understand it, so I guessed there had to be something to it.

"Mustn't oversimplify," warned Justin.

"If we sit still it could snowball," agreed Arnold.

"If the SEAT were compulsory, we could develop data to guide therapeutic interventions and stop things like this before they get started."

"Sometimes we simply need to put our hand down."

"How do they expect our sex-ed results to interface at the behavioral level if they drawdown our funding every year?"

"I don't intend to drop anchor until we're out of the woods!"

Entertained and appalled at the same time, I hadn't been paying attention to my bladder, which had been desperately trying to get my attention. When it finally "reached" me, it informed me that I had very little time left before I embarrassed myself. "I've got to go," I announced. "Back to class," I added, for the sake of decorum.

That seemed to wake Arnold from his trance: "YOU SHOULD HAVE GONE STRAIGHT TO YOUR CLASSROOM WHEN WE TOOK CHARGE. IF SOMETHING HAS HAPPENED IN YOUR ABSENCE, THE SCHOOL WILL BE SUED!"

Halfway down the hall, I heard Max call, "The union will stand behind you!"

Chapter 28

I phoned Vern three times that night. No answer. So I called Arnold at home. He said Vern was in the hospital.

"Hospital! I didn't think he was that bad."

"You're wrong about a lot things, Ms. Butler! I'm afraid he's going to sue the school"

"Is it his knee?"

"Apparently his heart. I don't see how he can sue us if as a result of this incident they discovered a potentially serious condition. He should be grateful. He could have died."

"Which hospital?"

"It was your idea to move him. You already had him on his feet when Dr. Sweet and I arrived. The schools are blamed for everything these days. But do we, in fact, get the funding to undo the harm that has already been done in the home? It didn't used to be this way."

"What way?"

"Goodbye, Miss Butler. I hope you feel better." He hung up. I called him back and asked again which hospital Vern was in.

"St. Joseph's."

Next day, I went to see him. He told me where to find his key, and I went to the store for him. I stocked his refrigerator.

The hospital sent him home a few days later, and he told me he wasn't going to work for a month.

I asked about his heart. He shrugged.

"They gave me some new pills and advised me to change my diet."

I gave him the double dickens for not telling Arnold that it was Didimo who beat him up.

"And what would happen if I told him? He'd start a file on the lad? He'd tell Jenny to counsel him? The boy's a psychopath. And Arnold is a ... I don't know what he is. But it has a number."

"In that case, forget him. Tell the police."

"And what will they do? It's my word against his. And my word is worth no more than his in our enlightened age. Even if they investigate, it will be weeks before anything happens—*if* anything happens. In the meantime, my friend Didimo, or one of his cohorts, will do me in."

"Oh, Vern, you exaggerate."

"No exaggeration, dear. Wake up and smell the cordite."

"Why does he bother coming to school? He never comes to class."

"He's recruiting honeybuns for his business. What? You don't know about that?"

"Oh, Vern, be sensible. Yes, I've heard Lyle and Max fantasize about some sort of teenage sex ring. But those guys are crazy. Lyle believes the world's coming to an end tomorrow—or at least by next week—and Max thinks ... Well, who knows what Max thinks? Now, I ask you, could a gang or a bevy or a troop or a whatever you want to call 'em of teenage prostitutes be operating at Pershing without somebody spilling the beans? It's just one more of those stupid rumors like the one about aliens landing in New Mexico."

"New Mexico *is* full of aliens."

"I mean … You know what I mean."

"Maybe the girls aren't selling themselves to their classmates. Maybe they're … "

"Vern. If a gang of high school girls were working the streets, one of them would have been arrested by now. Right? Right."

"Oh, you're so sensible, dear. That's why you're so out of it."

The TV weather person said it was almost spring. Maybe so, but there was still snow on the ground and my sinuses were still stopped up. I fed my cat. I scrubbed the bathroom. I ran the vacuum, and I told myself for the hundredth time that my parents' house was too big for me. Then I played the piano, making even more mistakes than usual. As a last resort, I went shopping.

A passing car splattered me with slush. And as I climbed a low mound of snow between the street and the sidewalk, I punched through a soft spot and sank to my knees. Snow fell into the tops of my boots. I got cold feet. That night I called Vern to ask him how he was (but really to tell him how miserable I was). He recommended a clove of garlic and a cup of ginger tea.

By the time the anniversary of my father's death rolled around, I felt better. Nevertheless, I told Shirley I would be out one more day.

"Are you still sick?"

"Yes," I said, agreeing to the lie that made it possible to run the system according to the rules. "If there are no more lesson plans in my desk, tell the sub to show a movie."

On the way to the cemetery, I stopped at The House of Flowers.

"Hello, my name is Butler. I ordered a . . ."

"Miss B.! It's you! Remember me? Randy Vespa, fifth period."

"Randy, of course," I replied automatically—but then I really did remember him. A very good writer, actually. I had urged him to consider journalism.

"Whatdayathink? Me and Terrell bought this place five years ago. Pretty nice, huh? Usually Terrell's here, too, but one of our kids is sick today, so she stayed home. She'll be sorry she missed you. We've got five, can you believe it? Twin girls, and three boys. But I told her, I said, 'Honey, that's it.' I said, 'How're we gonna keep track of all the grandkids?' I can't keep track of the ones we've got now. Here's your flowers. Miss B., Terrell musta told me a dozen times, you were the one who got her into writing. She does the newsletter for our church. It won a prize last year. Life is pretty funny, huh? Hey, I guess you never had a class like ours, huh? You ever find out what was in those brownies we gave you? Yeah? I thought so. You were pretty cool. But lissen, I learned more from you 'n anybody."

"What did you learn, Randy?"

"Hey, lots of stuff. You changed my whole life."

"Oh, surely not."

"You surely did. Remember me and Bobby Ickles—how we kept gettin' into trouble. You had to separate us. So you moved me over to sit by Terrell—your fave. And the rest, as they say, is history. We been married fifteen years. Don't seem possible does it?"

"That's wonderful, Randy. Good to see you. Be sure to tell Terrell hello."

"You have a nice day, Miss B."

I drove through the cemetery gate and along the access road to the top of the loop and parked. Carrying the spray I'd picked up at The House of Flowers, I walked down to the leafless honey locust and turned left. The ground was soft and spotted with patches of dirty, crusty snow. I wasn't surprised to be the only one there. It was a good day to be inside. So why wasn't I inside? I felt stupid. What difference did it make if I visited my parents' graves on this particular day or on some other day? Or if I "visited" their graves at all? Why didn't I just say a prayer for them while lying on the couch in my nice, warm house? That would be the sensible thing, wouldn't it?

At their graves, I stuck the wires at the bottom of my spray through a scrap of snow into the soft ground and stepped back. (They were buried on top of each other so I needed only one spray.) The flowers would fade unseen probably by anyone, and so what? I felt like a television journalist. I could hear myself saying, "This is Barbara Butler, speaking to you live from Bethel cemetery. Not much going on here, but we'll continue to monitor the situation. Back to you, Jack."

And just as some people are stricken by the conviction of guilt, I was stricken by the conviction of futility. I remembered some lines from a poem. What poem? I didn't know.

I must have memorized it in high school. We still memorized poems when I was in high school.

The gay will laugh
When thou art gone, the solemn brood of care
Plod on, and each one as before will chase
His favorite phantom; ...

Feeling like I ought to do something but not knowing what, I got down on one knee. But I didn't know what to say or think. All I knew for sure was that my knee was cold, and it was time for lunch.

Chapter 29

Walking back to my car, I saw I was not the only person at the cemetery that day after all. There was a man up ahead, squatting before a grave with one hand on the tombstone. As I got closer I saw—with mild alarm—that it was Mark Miles. What was he doing here? Was he following me? Why would he be doing that? But that was what detectives did, didn't they?—follow people?

I was getting as crazy as "the boys" in the faculty lounge.

No doubt he was there "to visit" someone, just like me. I slowed down and was about to start detouring around him but that proved unnecessary. He stood up and walked off towards a car that was parked on an access road.

As I watched him drive away. I told myself this had been my chance to tell him it was Didimo who beat up Vern. Yes, but it just hadn't seemed right—not in the cemetery. It would have been like talking business in church. That was what I told myself. But as I'm writing this I realize that that wasn't it at all. I didn't call out to him because I was too embarrassed to face him after the stupid fantasies I'd been having about him.

There was a Greek restaurant nearby. A man I used to know used to take me there. So that's where I went. As I walked in, I saw Mark again. He was sitting at a table, looking at a menu and flirting with a waitress. He saw me, too, so I couldn't turn around and walk out.

The waitress he'd been talking to walked away as I approached.

"Hi, remember me."

"My old English teacher."

"Try 'ex' or 'former,'" I said. "May I sit down?"

"I saw you at the cemetery," I said.

The waitress returned and we ordered.

"Was that you? I was surprised to see anybody else out on a day like this."

No ring, I noticed, but a lot of men don't wear them. My father didn't. My mother said none of her girlfriends had double ring ceremonies.

Then he asked, "Do you believe in God?"

Wow! That woke me from my reverie. It's perfectly all right these days to have your baby on television, or to teach masturbation to teenagers, but to ask somebody about God? Nobody did that. At least nobody I knew. All the people I knew were quite shy about God.

The waitress brought our orders, which gave me a moment to think. Not that it did me any good. "Yes," I said, "I do, I think."

He quoted, "'There is more to heaven and earth than is dreamt of in our philosophy, Horatio.' See, I learned something in your class after all."

This was like a conversation I was overhearing from somewhere else, not one I was actually part of. I heard myself saying appropriate things, but at the same time I was thinking about that teacher out in Oregon who went to prison for sleeping with one of her students. I forget the details, but if it was all right for a high school girl to have an abortion without even telling her parents, why was it against the law for a big strapping eighteen-year-old boy "to choose" to sleep with his teacher? Not that I wanted to sleep with any of my students. Good grief! I'd rather eat glass. But...

"Hey," he said, "I asked you a question."

Flustered, I said, "Sorry."

"Sorry's no reason."

Taken aback, I patted my mouth with my paper napkin.

He grinned. "Now, I'm the one who's sorry. That was something my mother used to say. She'd catch me doing something I shouldn't and I'd say 'I'm sorry,' and she'd say, 'Sorry's no reason.' When you said 'sorry,' it was just automatic." He shrugged and used his last French fry to draw a circle in the catsup on his plate. "Another thing, now that I think of it—she used to say, 'Just before the "at."' She'd tell me to go get something, and I'd say, 'Where's it at?' and she'd say, 'Just before the "at."' Okay, I understood that the 'it' was in front of the 'at.' But she acted like this was some big deal. I asked her about it once, but she brushed me off."

It was my turn to grin. I said, "Your English teacher didn't do a very good job, did she? There was a time when people thought we shouldn't end a sentence with a preposition."

"What's a preposition?"

"Surely you don't want an English lesson?"

"I guess not. So what did you want to talk to me about?"

I told him about Didimo beating up Vern.

"I hear you were at Kim Soo's the other night."

That caught me off balance. I said, "I didn't see you at the station."

"No, it's Herby Wilson's case, but we talk, you know. He says you say you didn't see anybody."

"No. I mean, yes, that's what I said. I didn't."

"Herby thinks it was maybe a couple of kids."

"Kids," I repeated.

He just looked at me.

"From Pershing, you mean?"

"Maybe."

"Can you," I asked Mark, "imagine any of the kids you went to school with robbing a store and shooting someone?"

"Times change."

I said, "Sometimes I have a hard time remembering my students are children."

"They aren't," he replied. "I don't know what they are. But they aren't children."

I made a mental note. "Children" was another one of those words along with "blackboard" and "school bell."

"So you think somebody from Pershing... That's unbelievable."

"Things can be unbelievable and still be true."

That struck me as profound. And then I realized what else he thought.

"You think whoever shot the clerk at Kim Soo's—that he may also be the person who killed Immaculata, right?"

"You know, we usually hear stuff about stuff like this. Somebody can't keep his mouth shut or somebody tips us off because he's pissed off at the shooter. But whoever did this has got everybody scared shitless. Er, I mean ... "

"It's all right. Permissible language has changed, too."

"Yeah. Well, I think Herby 'n me better have a talk with your friend, Vern. But, don't worry. I'll make up something about how we were tipped off. He won't know you told us."

"That's not necessary. Vern knows how I feel. This isn't just about him."

The waitress brought our check. I said I'd pay my share.

"Forget it."

"Nonsense."

"Listen," we both said at the same time.

"Jinks," I said.

He looked blank.

"Didn't you ever say that in grade school when you and somebody said the same word at the same time?"

I could see it coming back to him. "So," I said, offering him my little finger, curled and ready to be hooked.

Bemused, he linked his little finger to mine and we pulled to see who could pull the other person's finger straight. He let me win.

"What'd you wish?"

"If I tell it won't come true." I'm sure I was blushing.

"I sort of remember ... " he mused. "Something about cooties?"

"Oh, gosh yes. We had Cootie Kings and Cootie Queens. I had cootie-proof signs on my Keds and on all my books."

"Ring-a-levio," he muttered, with a far away look on his face. "Jeeze, I'd forgotten all about that stuff."

"Did you ever play clapping games?"

"Clapping games."

"Put your hands up, detective."

"Oh, yeah. Girl stuff."

But he did as he was told, and I took him through

> *Miss Mary Mack, Mack, Mack,*
> *All dressed in black, black, black,*
> *With silver buttons, buttons, buttons,*
> *Down her back, back, back.*
> *She went upstairs to make her bed.*
> *She made a mistake and bumped her head.*
> *She went downstairs to wash the dishes.*
> *She made a mistake and washed her wishes.*

She went outside to hang her clothes.
She made a mistake and hung her nose.

The regulars at the bar and the pretty waitresses were all looking at us.

"You're a little crazy, you know?" he said.

"I'm rubber. You're glue. Whatever you say bounces off me and sticks to you."

When he stopped laughing, he said, "Hey, I remember one. 'I see London. I see France...'"

We both grinned, and I almost asked him if he wanted to come see my paintings, but I didn't, thank goodness. It would have ruined everything.

Chapter 30

A spring blizzard buried parked cars and left tree branches sagging. Pershing closed for two days. But by the end of the week chunks of snow were sliding from roofs, rivulets of melted snow were running beside the curbs, and the wind was shaking life back into trees and bushes. On the way to work, I saw a long line of cars in front of a car wash.

Pressing down my fluttering skirt, I walked past the flagpole on my way to the building.

"Hey, Miss B., we gonna do anything t'day?"

"Hey, Butler, would you write me a letter for college?"

"Hey, y' write one fer her, ya gotta write one fer me, too!"

"Go away, Barney."

"Hey, I deserve a chance 's much 's her."

They were all so needy and so friendly. I accused myself of not liking them enough. But who could like them *enough*?

I went through the motions of teaching but I was on auto-pilot. So were my students. We were all counting the days until school was out. But the bureaucratic wheels continued to turn. Mossman stopped me in the hall to bring to my attention that Dr. Pisapus had brought to his attention that my Absent/Tardy Reports had been full of errors lately. And where, pray tell, was my Furniture and Equipment Inventory? Then Jenny stopped me to ask if something was bothering me. She thought there might be, because I had failed to respond to her greeting last Friday.

"Hi," said Clara Dingle as she sat down beside me in the auditorium. "So who's going to get cutest couple? Pippy Ng and Hugh Horomer deserve it. But I hear the hoody element is voting for Lance and that Debbie who works in the library. They haven't been going together long enough in my opinion."

When I failed to reply, she touched my arm. "What's your opinion?"

I heard her, but I didn't reply because I was psyching myself up to do what I had decided to do.

Clara tried a new subject. "How's Vern? I think it's wonderful that you two are friends."

That got my attention. "What's wonderful about it?"

"We're all different in different ways," she said, with a knowing look. "Maybe we should have a welcome home party for him."

"I doubt if Vern thinks of Pershing as his home."

"Oh, you know what I mean. Wait! Where are you going?"

"Up on the stage. I have to give an award."

After school, I stopped by the main office to check my box. Shirley stopped typing and beckoned.

"What is it, Shirley?"

"Grammar question. That word. You know, that word. I'm typing this incident report for Dr. Mossman, and he says I have to write it out, but is it two words or one? Or is it hyphenated? What's right?"

"What word, Shirley?"

She tugged at my sleeve. I bent closer. "Mother-um-uker." she whispered.

Before I could speak, her phone rang and she answered it.

Clara came over, dragging Ralph with her. "Barbara! Ralph, here, has a great idea. Tell her, Ralph."

"Well, we got this pink pass problem, agreed? Me, I make two copies, but lots of people don't, okay? So why can't we have pads be made up like those old fashioned receipts. Know what I mean? With carbon paper in between each sheet. That way when we wrote a pink pass, we'd have a record. What do you think?"

"You told me your idea before, Ralph. I have to go home now."

"No, really, if we all got behind it, we could get something accomplished around here."

I gently pushed him aside. But Arnold, Jenny, and Justin were standing between me and the door, conferring about something. When Jenny saw me coming, she said something to the others. They all looked at me.

"Excuse me," I said. But nobody moved.

"I hope you're happy," blustered Arnold. "What must our students think?"

"Mrs. Clambering will probably sue us," said Jenny. "I wouldn't be surprised."

"Why would she do that, Jenny?"

"It's not fair," intoned Justin, solemnly.

I pretended not to know what had upset them. "Why would Mrs. Clambering sue us?"

"Well," said Jenny, "because Eddy didn't get the reading award. Everybody knows Johnson isn't college material, so how could she possibly deserve an award for loving books?"

"Fairness," sputtered Arnold. "Fairness. Fairness. Is she the role model we should be propagating? No, she's not. I'm told she refused to better herself—rejected a basketball scholarship. What were you thinking, Barbara? What? What?"

Behind me, Shirley called out, "That was Mr. Harmon. He'll be back on Monday."

Chapter 31

I took my first period to the library and asked Ms. Riddle to watch them for a minute.

"That's not my job. I'm not a teacher. It's against the rules!"

"I'll be right back."

I had expected to catch Vern in the main office before school, but he must have gone straight to his room. That's where I was headed, but before I got there, I came upon Appaloosa and another girl sitting on the floor, their backs against the wall.

"What are you two doing out here?"

"Mince kicked us out."

"Said we was talkin'."

Not my business, I told myself and went on down the silent hall. When I opened the door to Vern's room, I felt like I'd entered an alternative universe. Students were yelling and dancing. Music was blaring. Balloons were tied to deskchairs. What was left of a cake littered Vern's desk. "WE LOVE YOU" was printed on one board; "WELCOME HOME," on another.

"STOP THAT!" I bellowed at two boys who were kicking ice cubes back and forth across the floor. There was a cooler in the corner and empty soda cans lined the chalk rail.

"Maynard," I shouted, grabbing a boy I recognized. "Where's Mr. Harmon?"

"We're having a party for him."

"Yes, but where is he?" The boy shrugged and pulled away. I had to get back to my own class, but I couldn't leave those kids. They were wild. I decided I had to notify the office and pressed the intercom button.

"Hello? Hello? This is Miss Butler."

"Who?" said Shirley's voice. "Isn't this Mr. Harmon's room?"

"Yes, Shirley, but he's not here. Send somebody up here who can take his class."

Eventually, Arnold himself arrived. He wanted to know why I'd sent all those girls out in the hall. I kept telling him Mr. Harmon was missing,

"Who authorized this party? Does the office know about this party?"

Shirley's voice came over the intercom: "Dr. Windmuller? The plumbers are here."

He pressed the button and shouted into the speaker, "Not now, Shirley!"

"I'm leaving," I said. "I have a class in the library."

"Leaving? You can't. It's not professional."

"Dr. Windmuller," said Shirley. "The central office is on the phone. It's about Save the Earth Day."

He pressed the button. "Tell Dr. Sweet."

He released the button. Shirley said, "He's not here."

He pressed the button again. "Dr. Mossman then."

He released the button.

"He's about a fight in the gym."

"I've got to get back to my class," I repeated.

"No, no!" he bleated. Then shouting at the intercom, he said, "Shirley, I've got too many balls in the fire right now, and … Miss Butler! Stop! You can't leave … "

But I did. And outside in the hall, I found fifteen or twenty girls standing outside Mince's room.

"What's going on?"

A giggly girl said, "She does it all the time."

"Who? Does what?"

"Look," commanded the girl, taking my arm and drawing me to the small window in the classroom door.

Inside the room, Gladys was standing in front of rows of empty deskchairs. Her mouth was moving. She was teaching to an empty room. I turned back and looked at the girls. They grinned. I couldn't leave them out there in the hall, could I? Not your problem, I scolded myself, silently. What makes you think everything is your problem? I left them there.

Halfway down the stairs to the library, I met Clara coming up. Raising her head, she saw me and blocked my way.

"He ran off. Wouldn't listen. My girls baked him a cake. Why was he so mad?"

I said I was in a hurry, faked left, and tried to go right. She blocked me. I faked right and tried to go left. She blocked me again, extending her arms. "It's his self-hatred," she declared. "We have to overcome it."

I lifted her left arm and ducked under it.

"What's wrong?" she called after me. "What's wrong? I don't understand you."

Chapter 32

During my free period, I phoned Vern's apartment No answer. After school I called him from home. No answer. I tried again after dinner. Nothing. So I put on a raincoat, got out my umbrella and set off.

I knocked on his door and waited. I pressed his buzzer and waited. Idly, I tried the door. To my surprise, it opened.

"Hey! Vern? It's me!"

No answer. "Yoo-hoo!" I called, thinking maybe he'd fallen or fainted or something.

"I've got a gun!" he shouted hoarsely from another room.

"Vern, it's me."

"YOU!" he roared, leaping into view like a ballet dancer coming on stage. He had on a wig, a slip, a wrapper, and was brandishing a large kitchen knife.

"Nobody asked you here!"

"Vern, I'm dripping. Where can I put this?"

I brandished my umbrella.

He went right on waving that damn knife and yelling, "Nobody allowed backstage! Nobody allowed backstage!"

Disconcerted, I dropped my umbrella, and when I stooped to pick it up, I knocked over a vase that was on a little table.

"Oh, I'm sorry," I said, looking up just in time to see him lunging at me. He said later that he was going to help me clean up the mess, but it didn't seem that way to me at the time. Leaning backwards to avoid the knife, I fell over, and rolled to one side. Snapping open my purse, I pulled out Arnold's gun.

"GET BACK!"

He froze, but was still bending over me and still holding the knife.

Then he stepped back, and I got to my feet.

He lowered his arms and pointed at the gun. "Is that real?"

When I looked where he was pointing, he stepped forward and twisted the gun from my hand.

"Give it back. It's not yours."

"But, darling, this is just what I need."

He aimed at an imaginary intruder and said, "Da! Da! Da!"

"Vern, give it back, and I'll go."

"I thought you were Didimo."

"Do I sound like Didimo?"

"I've been thinking about him a lot."

"Why didn't you tell the police what he did to you?"

"THE POLICE! They came here. Two of them. And YOU! You told them, didn't you! It had to be you!"

I tried to divert him by singing softly, "It had to be me, wonderful me. It ha-a-ad to be me," as I danced sedately. Vern normally appreciates that sort of thing, but not that night.

"If he hears about it, it will be your fault! If he kills me, YOU'LL be to blame."

"Vern, be careful! I think that thing's loaded"

"Oh, foolish Vern. Careless little Vern. Can't be trusted. Who asked you to look after me?"

"Vern, you're not being fair. When I went by your room this morning..."

"Oh, were you on the reception committee?"

"I didn't know anything about it, but when you weren't there, I…"

"Darling Clara."

"She was just trying to be nice," I said, unable to look away from the gun he was waving from side to side. "Arnold is furious with you," I added. "He wants to fire you for leaving school without telling anyone."

"He can't fire me. The union won't let him. Look how long he's been trying to fire Sitwell. Stay back!"

"Vern, Vern, you're acting like a teenager."

"Well, you're acting like my mother."

It was hopeless. I could see that. But I couldn't leave without my gun. "I've got a headache," I said. "Do you have any aspirin?" And then I noticed what I should have seen right off. There were two wine glasses on the coffee table. Vern had company. I had interrupted them. That was why he hadn't heard me knocking.

So where was he—the other person? Or was it a "she"? The bedroom? The bathroom? The kitchen? I glanced about, embarrassed and angry at the same time. It was all so crazy! And then I gave up. I slumped back on the couch and started weeping. I'd had all the craziness I could take.

"What's wrong?" he asked, sitting down beside me.

"Everything."

"Oh, that," he said. "That's been bothering me, too."

He put the gun on the coffee table, plucked a Kleenex from a little box, and blotted the tears from my cheeks.

I was confused by his sudden alteration but coherent enough to retrieve my gun. He didn't react. I slipped it in my purse.

He leaned back, shut his eyes, and sighed.

"Vern, what's wrong?"

"You think I'm a pervert."

"A what? Oh, Vern, be serious."

"I disgust you. I disgust everybody."

"Vern, that's stupid. Listen, I have to be going. It's a school night, you know."

All at once he went crazy again.

"So I'm stupid, too. You said so. You make me nauseous."

"Nauseous?" I queried. "Oh, surely not." And in my best Miss Nitpicky voice, I told him: "'Nauseous' is an adjective. So if you say I make you 'nauseous,' what you are saying is that I transform you into a person who makes other people want to vomit. But what you want to say is that I make *you* want to vomit, right? Yes, so what you should say is, 'I nauseate you.' There's quite a difference." I smiled snottily.

For a moment his mouth opened and closed silently. Then he snarled, "Well, aren't we perfect?"

I raised my eyebrows high enough to lift me off the floor and turned to leave.

He said nobody cared about "that crap" anymore, so at the door, I paused to say, "If you're so afraid of Didimo, you might try locking your door."

"Maybe the reason I forgot is that I'm so afraid of him I can't think straight!"

"And maybe you are just nuts," I said. I'd had it with him.

"Oh, yes, let's psychoanalyze stupid, perverted Vern. Maybe I want Didimo to murder me—to put me out of my misery."

"Good night, Vern."

"Did you hear me? Let's consult with Dr. Sweet. He's a transactional analyst. He can explain everything. He has a credential. What he can't do is to imagine..."

I pulled the door shut.

Driving home, I realized he was right. And not just about Sweet. I wasn't much better. Could I imagine Vern? Nor really. Or anybody else at Pershing. My students especially. And how could I teach them if I couldn't imagine them? I tried to imagine Kiesha's life outside of my classroom and drew a blank. I tried to imagine Appaloosa's. Another blank. Self-indulgently, I let myself imagine for a moment what a great teacher I'd be if I had complete charge of their screwed-up, stunted lives. The Great Dictator! But then I saw that all I would do would be to turn out various versions of my self-blessed self, and who would want a world full of me's? Not me, certainly. Especially not me. Maybe I could help them if I were allowed to drill them on a few basic things, but I wasn't. Nobody agreed on what was basic anymore.

It wasn't like I hadn't thought things like this before. I had. Many times. But I was tired of pretending, tired of trying to get along with the unimaginable people in the faculty lounge, tired of trying to force my unimaginable students to learn whatever the unimaginable pipsqueak poobahs of the Department of Education decided they should.

I can't be more specific, but, looking back, I think it was something in the tone of Vern's voice that made me make up my mind.

Chapter 33

I didn't have a suitable box for Arnold's gun. So I decided to go shopping after school and buy something that came in a suitable box.

But first I had to have lunch with Vern. I wanted to make-up—so did he.

I took my lunch down to his room. Our free periods coincided. I said I was sorry I'd barged into his apartment when he had company.

He explained that he hadn't had company. "Vern" had just been entertaining "Fern."

"We like to talk things over now and then."

I said I was sorry anyhow, and he forgave me, but said he was still mad at me for "betraying" him to the police.

"I'm sure you will be very sorry if Didimo rubs me out. I, on the other hand, will be dead."

I told him he was letting his imagination run away with him. I said, "I agree with you that boy is bad news, but..."

"Didimo is not a 'boy'!" he snarled.

And then he told me about being interviewed by Mark and Herb.

"They were so polite! It was unnerving. I mean, it was just so ominous."

As I've said, Vern likes to dramatize. In any case, they told him straight out that they wanted an excuse to arrest Didimo and search his house—his mother's house, that is. So Vern suggested they put some marijuana in his pocket and say they found it, like in the movies. They ignored that idea. They wanted Vern to bring charges against him. He refused. I think he likes feeling scared as long as he isn't too really scared. It's part of his feminine persona.

He told them he didn't know who beat him up, but they knew he knew, and he knew they knew he knew.

They promised to protect him, but he didn't trust them. He fantasized about quitting his job and going to another town where he could be Fern all the time. A new life. Nobody would be able to find him. But he couldn't do that. He couldn't afford to quit his crappy job at Pershing because if he did, he'd lose his seniority and make maybe half as much money as a new hire. Besides he hadn't saved anything. Just before I arrived at his apartment, "Fern" had been blaming him for not putting anything aside for their retirement, and then I came along. The perfect scapegoat.

When I started back to my room, there were hardly any students in the hall, which meant the second bell was about to ring. We hugged and I hurried upstairs.

Later, I remembered what he said about Didimo not being "a boy," that is to say, "a child." He was right, of course. So obvious when you think about it. But what was he then? What do we call a Didimo? A student? Ha-ha! A minor? Possibly, in a legal sense. But, really, "a minor" was not what he was. He was a major—a major headache.

We need a new language.

Chapter 34

I found a box for Arnold's gun and nested it in wadded newspaper. Then I wrapped the box in brown paper and took it to school. I was sick and tired of the stupid thing. What were my alternatives? I could have thrown it in a river, if there had been a convenient river, which there wasn't. I could have given it to Mark, but if I did that, Arnold might have gotten into trouble, and I didn't want to get him into trouble, although I was sure he had a license for the damn thing. Arnold would never do anything illegal.

I was the one who might have gotten into trouble. After all, I'd stolen it.

Phil Sitwell greeted me as I walked into the main office. "Mornin' Barb. What are you on?"

"Edge."

"How's that? Oh, I getcha. Well, we're all on somethin'. Everybody needs little boost the last month. It's Librium for

Lavender. Valium for ol' Max. And we all know what Arnold's on—food. He's lookin' like one of them Japanese wrestlers. How much you think he's gained?"

Stepping away from the reek of his mouthwash, I said, "Thank God, I'm not coming back next year."

"You're not? How come?"

"I'd rather wait tables," I said, flippantly, and turned to speak to Shirley, but she was watering her violets and Clara was asking her if she wanted to trade a leaf from her Frilly Billy for one from a Little Rogue.

"People around here don't ask," complained Shirley. "They just take. Ook ad dim. Pour iddle guy." And then she turned to me and asked, "How would you like it if somebody came along and broke one of your arms off?"

I said, "Shirley, do you have any..."

But Gladys Mince had heard what I said to Phil. She seized my wrist and hissed, "No! No! An educated person like yourself—you don't have to wait tables!" Then, almost shouting, she said, "GET A JOB IN A PRIVATE SCHOOL! DON'T PUT UP WITH TOM, DICK, AND HARRY. STAY AWAY FROM THOSE THREE—DICK, TOM, AND HARRY!" Shocked by her own vehemence, she slid her eyes from side to side, released my arm, and toddled away.

"Morning, Barby," said Lyle, and grasping Max's arm, he turned him towards me. "Say hello to Barby, Max."

But before Max could speak, Justin Sweet emerged from his office and called out, "Don't forget to vote!"

Everyone stopped talking and looked at him. He smiled uneasily, stepped backwards slowly, and pulled the door shut after him.

"I think he means the school bond levy," someone said.

"Did that pass?"

"No, the vote's today."

"What's the use? Parents don't care about their kids anymore," declared Lyle.

Belatedly, the chemically altered Max Tinder boomed, "WONDERFUL weather. WONDERFUL!"

Shirley turned on him and snapped, "You won't think it was so wonderful if somebody broke one of your arms off!"

"I'M GOING TO MY ROOM NOW!" announced Max.

But he didn't. He stood there picking his nose and examining what he found in it.

Phil nudged me, "Spring has sprung," he giggled.

People started leaving the office to go to class. I pretended to be reading something I'd taken from my mailbox. When I was sure no one was looking, I slipped the package containing the gun into Arnold's mailbox.

Then someone touched me on my shoulder and I nearly jumped out of my skin. It was Jenny. She looked at me with that woebegone look of hers and asked me, "What are we going to do? He's getting worse."

Realizing I hadn't been caught, I recovered and assured her, "Don't worry. He's going to be fine."

"How can you be sure?"

"Ah, well . . . Because the semester's over. "

"Do you really think that will make him better?"

I went upstairs to my room.

A paper airplane crashed on my desk.

"Hey don't wad it up, Miss B. That's my property," a boy protested.

"Ain't no bell yet, Miss Butler. We do what we want till the bell."

The bell buzzed. I stood up and said, "All right class..."
But my voice was overridden by a voice from the intercom.

"Good morning, students. This is your principal speaking with today's special announcements."

I listened closely. But I could tell from his voice that he hadn't found it yet, so I applied myself to my Absent/Tardy Report while he made his announcements.

"Today we congratulate Tina Biesanz for her winning slogan in the Citizenship Contest. Her slogan is: 'Don't mess up your head with grass. / Concentrate on your grade in class.' Congratulations, Tina. Congratulations go also to our wrestlers who clobbered Bishop McGuire last night. Congratulations, Mat-men. Returning you now to your classroom instructor. And remember: 'Concentrate on your grades, class. / Don't let the opportunities go past.'"

"'Friday is Senior rebellion day,'" I announced, reading aloud from the Bulletin. "'Students may dress as they wish but have to wear shoes. It's a health department rule.'" I scanned the room. No one was listening. They were signing each other's yearbooks. Carmen laid hers in front of me and asked me to sign it.

I looked at what her friends had written: "The day you wore your green blouse, you made me your rock solid friend" and "I'll never forget the day you sharpened my pencil for me."

"Yeah," Carmen explained. "That's how they do now. They try to write somethin' incriminatin'."

"Yes, Darlene, what is it?"

"Can I hava pass? I wanna get Mossman t' sign my book."

"She's gonna get Monster Man to sign her yearbook!" jeered Eddy, looking around for support from the rest of the class. But nobody paid any attention. Chastened, he asked Darlene, "Why do you want him to sign it?"

Arching her back and looking at him with calculated sultriness, she drawled, "Because Ed-dee, he is so totally hot!"

"Yeah, and totally forty," observed Carmen, her friendly rival.

"New haircut, Carmen? Who cut it?"

Lance brought me a letter he'd written to his grandfather who lived in California. He wanted to know if it was "all right."

"Well, you misspelled 'receive' and 'friend.'"

"Yeah, but is it okay?"

"And 'opportunity.'"

"Wha? Where?"

"It's 'o-r' not 'u-r.'"

"No!"

"Look it up."

"Shee. Forget it. All I wanted was is it all right."

Nan Wang told him if he phoned his grandfather he wouldn't need to spell anything.

I gave a test to every class that day. I graded the tests from first period while the kids in second were taking theirs, not that it mattered. I'd already assigned their semester grades. But by giving them a test, I kept them quiet. When I needed a break, I poured myself a cup of cold coffee from my thermos. Sipping it, I thought about how I'd changed Randy Vespa's whole life by moving him away from Bobby Ickles and making him sit next to Terrill. Would I have done that if I'd known they would get married? How many other kids had I influenced without having the slightest idea what I was doing?

Alan Stickler finished first. "Sure hope I get an 'A,'" he said, tossing his test on my desk.

I sighed and said, "If you started your sentences with capitals and ended them with periods, you did fine."

"WHA? WHA?" he exploded.

I pushed off from my desk and let my chair roll backwards to put some distance between us.

"You goofed!" he accused, leaning over my desk. "You never told us about that."

"Never told us about what?" inquired several voices.

"ALAN, SIT DOWN!" I said firmly. "Everyone be quiet and finish your test."

When they were finished, I went over the answers with them but, as usual, we veered off the subject. Alan began his familiar argument that we had to colonize Mars.

I told him, "Alan, if I've told you once, I've told you a million times that argument by analogy doesn't work. Just because Europeans colonized America doesn't mean we will be able to colonize Mars."

Then from the back of the room came the unfamiliar voice of Herm the Germ: "Hey, them Puritans—I betcha some of them said, 'Hey, so we made it to Holland. That don't mean we can make it to America.'"

I was just swallowing a sip of coffee and had to choke it back to keep from spraying it all over. When I got it down, I started laughing. And I couldn't stop. The class watched me curiously. I noticed their attentiveness as, bleary eyed and weak, I struggled to compose myself. Then Carl Arkwright sauntered over to the door and looked out its little window.

"Your clock must be broke, Miss Butler. The other classes are out a'ready."

"Yeah," chimed in another boy, also standing up, "You better let us out or we'll miss our buses."

"S-sit down," I ordered hoarsely.

"SHE SAID WE COULD GO!" shouted a boy. "GO! GO!"

About a third of them went. A moment later, the bell buzzed, and the rest of them followed. With my eyes still teary, I sat at my desk taking deep breaths. I felt too frail and weak even to resent the way they'd taken advantage of me. When I recovered, I took out my grade book and changed The Germ's final grade from a "C," which he didn't deserve but needed to graduate, to a "B," which was absurd—the only "B" he ever made, I'm sure. But I have a weakness for people who make me laugh.

When I got to the main office after school, Arnold was there talking to Shirl and Jen. He was telling them about his dogs—he had two—and displaying all his old animation. His dogs had been a great comfort to him, he said.

I glanced at his mailbox. The package was gone.

"This last semester was a doozy, wasn't it?"

He was grinning and chuckling and sweating.

Shirl handed him a Kleenex.

Daubing his forehead, he said, "But we made it, didn't we?" He looked at us and giggled. "We got through it, didn't we? Hey, Barb, would I offend your feminist sensibilities if I said, 'You look great'? Doesn't she look great, Jenny? Not that you don't look great, too. And you, too, Shirley. Everybody looks great. I hope you stay in touch, Barb. We can always use another name on the substitute list."

I turned to Jen and asked, as if I didn't know, "What's happened to him?"

"He is much livelier, isn't he?"

I've heard there is a rule for writers of fiction that says if a gun is hanging on the wall over the fireplace in chapter one, it has to go off before the story ends. I felt like I'd entered a story when I stole Arnold's gun. But I hadn't. The story never really got going. And now there was no longer any possibility that it would.

Chapter 35

O n the last day of school, my students cheered and crowded out of my classroom into the hall, which was filled with the students from all the other classes who were talking and teasing and singing as they ambled from the building. Free! Free at last!

But not me. The faculty had to come back for another half-day. So the next morning I showed up to clean out my desk and turn in my grades. I was strolling about my room to stretch my legs when I noticed something funny about a row of paperbacks in the bookcase. I took one out. It fell apart in my hands. Someone had slit its spine with a razor. I took out another. Same thing. A goodbye gesture from someone whose self-esteem I had not adequately nurtured.

Pawing the mutilated books from the shelf, I left them on the floor for the janitor to throw away. Then, seeing it was almost eleven-thirty, I picked up the box of office supplies that I was awarding myself for many years of good and faithful service and headed downstairs to sign out.

Teachers were lounging about the main office, eyeing the clock. "See you next year," someone said to someone.

"I hope not," someone replied.

Max asked Jenny, "Going anywhere this summer?"

"No, I'm just going to lay around."

"How much do you intend to charge?" I asked as I passed by—a completely gratuitous bit of snottiness which had absolutely no effect on Jenny. I doubt if she ever knew there is a difference between "lie" and "lay," not that it matters to anyone anymore—except to dinosaurs like me. But this was my last day. I was tired of deferring to everyone's fragile self-esteem. Whatever happened to the idea of being cruel in order to be kind? I suspect that except for a few eccentrics like myself, the only people who still "get" that idea are in the military. Behind me, Max asked Clara if she knew "the corporations" were planning to take over the schools. "Yeah, they set up these charter schools, see, to drain our best students, and then they indoctrinate them. Yeah, to buy their sponsors' brands. It's all about sales, see. Read it in your Union newsletter, baby."

Out in the hall, I came upon Appaloosa and two boys I didn't know. "What are you guys doing here? School's out, remember?"

"Aw, we're helpin' Mince move her stuff. You seen her ankles? What makes 'em fat like that?"

Chapter 36

The Green Meadows Mall dominates the southwest suburbs the way cathedrals used to dominate towns in the middle ages. I entered it through a store that sold garden statues and walked out onto the main promenade where I accepted a discount certificate from an aggressive clown and sat down beside a fountain. I couldn't remember what I'd come to buy. After nine months of teaching school, I was too frazzled to keep my mind on anything. I decided to stroll around, hoping something would remind me of why I was there.

At Barnes and Noble, I came face to face with Eddy Clambering and a woman I took to be his mother.

"Hello, Eddy."

"Oh, hi, Miss Butler."

He was not happy to see me.

His mother held out her hand: "Hello. I'm Martha Clambering, Eddy's mother."

"Glad to meet you, Martha. I'm Barbara Butler, his English teacher."

She was distracted by her son. "Eddy, what's the matter with you?"

Cringing behind her, he was squirming and trying to

mouth a message to me without his mother's knowledge. I had no idea what he was trying to say.

"Straighten up, Eddy." She jerked his arm. "What are you doing?"

"Lookin' for a book, Momma," he said in a strangled voice, and stooped to search the lower shelves.

I watched him curiously. His mother was getting impatient. I tried to smooth things over by saying the usual things teachers say to a student's parent: "A pleasure to have had Eddy in class," blah, blah. And she said the usual things that a parent says to her child's teacher: "Eddy learned so much in your class," blah, blah.

We were both wondering what he was up to.

A bit coolly, his mother said she fully understood my initial reluctance to reevaluate Eddy's grade. She, too, of course, was very much in favor of strict standards. But Eddy really had misunderstood my questions, so it was only fair that he get a second chance. "When Mrs. Lavender called and told me you had agreed to let her retest Eddy in her office, I was so relieved. She's a lovely person, isn't she? So helpful."

I hope I controlled my expression. So Eddy had gotten his "A," after all. I tried to work up some indignation towards Jenny—and towards Arnold. She wouldn't change a grade without getting his permission. But the old spark wasn't there. What difference did it make?

"Here. This one," said Eddy, straightening up and showing me a copy of *The Great Gatsby*.

I could tell Martha Clambering thought her son and I had something going on between us that she didn't know about, but actually I was as much in the dark as she was.

"No," she said. "*This* is the book you're going to read, young man." She showed him the book she was holding: *On Your Way: How to Succeed in College.*

"I will, Momma. But I gotta read this book, too—er, again."
He looked desperately at me, hoping that I understood what
he was saying, which seemed to me to be something more
than just that he would actually read *Gatsby*. But who knows
what goes on in the mind of a teenager? I don't. I don't even
understand what goes on in my own mind. I was feeling a surprising surge of sympathy for the boy. I could remember how
I felt when I was his age. Nobody understood me—or wanted
to—and everything was potentially embarrassing. Everything.

Eddy's mother was saying, "If you've read that book,
you don't need to read it again. You don't have time to waste,
young man. You do not."

"N-no, I know, but this book. It's worth it. Isn't it, Miss
Butler? I'm gonna read it, um, again. I definitely am."

Before I could think what to say, I heard people shouting my name.

Darlene and Carmen, who were strolling through the
mall, had spotted me. They came charging into the bookstore,
waving the ice cream cones, and almost knocking over the
sign that said, "No Food Inside This Store."

"MISS B.! MISS B.!— Hi, Eddy.—HEY MISS B.! DIDJA
HEAR? DIDJA HEAR?"

Eddy's mother drew him closer to her.

He squirmed away from her.

The girls were licking their cones almost as fast as they
were talking. "Kiesh? She hadder baby. A girl! It's a girl!"

"And guess what her name is? Guess! Guess!"

"Didja hear what she named her?"

"We have to be going, Eddy. Glad to have met you, Miss
Butler. Come along, son."

"Bye, Eddy," chorused the girls.

"Eddy, come along."

"Hey, Eddy, you'd look good with an earring," called Darlene, naughtily, and was rewarded by a perceptible increase in the jerkiness of his mother's movements as she hustled him away.

"PEARL!" shrieked Carmen, "That's what she named her. Like in that book you read us."

"The baby of that woman with the 'A,'" added Darlene.

"I wish I was named after somebody in a book," said Carmen. "That'ud be cool."

Chapter 37

I sat in my studio (my parents' bedroom) drinking a second cup of coffee. I was five days into my retirement and still getting used to it. I was so glad I'd been able to retire early. So glad I would never have to teach another class. I was especially glad I'd gotten rid of Arnold's gun. Until it was gone, I hadn't realized how stressful it was to have it around.

A breeze was drifting through the open windows. Birds were flitting, squealing, and trilling, and long, early morning shadows lay across the lawn.

I stood up and walked around the room, looking at my paintings. They looked back at me. (We do a lot of that.)

There was only one little cloud in my big blue sky. I was beginning to regret agreeing to my brother's desire to sell the house. Where else was I going to find all this space? The phone rang. It was Amanda. She and Spence were going to a funeral that afternoon. Their sitter had canceled. Would I take care of Tanya for a few hours? I said sure and told her Ruthy was coming by. She didn't know about Ruthy, so I had to explain that she was the little sister of the girl who had been murdered, and that I had been tutoring her.

"She and Tanya are about the same age. It will be like a play-date for them."

Hearing myself say "play-date" surprised me. I'm sure I had never said it before. Why would I? I have no children. I was sure my mother never said it, either. When I was a girl, teenagers had "dates." Little kids just went outside and played with anybody they could find. Today it's the little kids who have "dates" and the teenagers who go outside and play with anybody they can find.

After lunch, I cleaned my brushes and took a book out to my screened-in front porch to wait for Ruthy. She was just coming up the porch steps when a strange car stopped in front of my house. Kiesha Johnson got out. As Ruthy and I watched, she leaned back into the car and pulled out her baby. I wasn't too surprised. Occasionally a student comes back to see me for reasons that are never clear to either of us. I assumed that Kiesha wanted to show me little Pearl. And it occurred to me that it would be good for Ruthy and Tanya to see a baby. A teachable moment. Maybe they could help change a diaper. Then, when Kiesha left, I could point out to them what folly it was for girls to have a baby without husbands to help them. Ruth and I stood at the screen door to greet her.

But as Kiesh came closer, I saw her shirt was torn, there was a scrape on her forehead, and her face was swollen around one eye.

"Good grief, Kiesh! What happened?"

I felt Ruthy edge behind me, pulling a little at my skirt.

"Oh, uh, nothin'. I—I fell down."

I was trying to remember where I'd put the card with Mark's number on it.

"I fell down," she repeated.

"Pretty bad fall."

"Yeah. Bad."

I wanted to say, "Cut the crap. What happened?" But I didn't. I assumed she would tell me when she was ready. I "gave her time," as the counselors say. And after warning Ruthy with a look not to say anything about our visitor's face, I oo-ed and ah-ed over little Pearl, just like everything was normal.

"I think she need changin'," said Kiesha, as if it were my fault.

"You can do it here," I said, clearing off the table on the porch. "Would you like a glass of ice tea?"

I took Ruthy with me into the kitchen and told her...I've forgotten what I told her, but she cut me off.

"Her boyfriend beat her up, didn't he?"

I just looked at her. What did she know about boyfriends who beat up their girlfriends? But this wasn't the time to ask. I said, "Maybe, but let's not say anything about it right now, okay?"

"Okay."

Then I told her she was going to have a playmate that afternoon, a little girl named Tanya. "My niece."

"What's a 'niece'?"

I explained as we walked back to the porch carrying glasses and a pitcher of ice tea. Kiesha was sitting on the glider. Little Pearl was on her lap, and the glider was squeaking as they slid back and forth.

Amanda drove up. I met her and Tanya halfway up the walk. I gave Tanya a kiss and stroked her hair while actually addressing myself to Amanda. I told her an ex-student of mine and her baby were up on the porch and told them to act like nothing was wrong. "I'll explain it all later," I said.

Then we went up the steps to the porch and I introduced Tanya to Ruthy, who immediately asked her if she could play the piano. They went inside and while they were pounding out a four-hand version of "Chopsticks," Amanda whispered to me that my visitor needed to go to one of those shelters for battered women.

"I know. I'm going to put her in touch with a detective I know."

"A detective? Barb, you've been holding out on us."

"Not really," I said.

Kiesha looked nervously at Amanda, then drew me aside and asked if we could talk.

I gave Amanda a look. She understood and said she had to be going. "Thanks for taking Tanya," she said, standing up and slinging her purse over her shoulder. But she didn't leave right away. The girls were in the kitchen checking out the refrigerator. She was waiting to tell Tanya goodbye.

I told Kiesha, "Come with me," and led her upstairs to my studio. We looked at my pictures while she jiggled Pearl. Then I told her she wasn't fooling me. I knew somebody had beaten her up, and I wanted to know who it was.

She ignored me and said, "I wisht I could paint pitchers—or jes', you know, do something."

"Would you like to learn to paint?"

(I had retired officially from teaching, but old habits die hard.)

She didn't respond. Little Pearl sucked on her bottle and waved her tiny feet. I motioned for Kiesha to sit in my father's old club chair. I sat on the stool in front of my easel. "Kiesh?" I prompted, "Tell me what happened. You didn't just fall."

Then she blurted, "Could you kinda like keep her for a couple a days?" which was not what I had been waiting to hear, and, tired of fooling around, I demanded to know who had beaten her up.

"Only for a day or two," she said, again ignoring my question.

"Why don't you leave her with your mother?"

"I can't. He knows where we live."

"Who is he?"

"You don't understand."

Ah, but I did. I had read books about battered women, and I was flooded with the certainty that I could help this girl. I felt advice and instructions forming in my mind like liberating armies. I could teach her to make something of herself. I could teach her how to dress and talk, and be a mother. She could be the daughter I never had. I could teach her how to get a job and be promoted, and live a reasonably happy life. I'd read books about all those things.

But when I saw the stubborn, sullen expression on her face, I also saw, in my mind's eye, my own overweening pedagogical triumphalism and realized that while I understood many things, I did not understand her, which was the main thing. And the only way I could ever understand her would be to become an intimate part of her life, something that—when I came right down to it—I was not willing to do—was not actually even capable of doing. Everyone has a certain range of people they can relate to. Mine is quite limited.

"Okay, Kiesh, I don't understand, but somebody beat you up! I understand that much. And so you want to leave Pearl with me because whoever did it is still after you, right? And you're afraid he'll hurt her, right? That's it, isn't it? Now look, This Will Not Do. No. If you want me to help you, you have to…" And inspired, I asked, "Was it Didimo?"

Jumping up, she pressed Pearl against her chest, and began patting her—but too hard and too rapidly. Pearl began to wail. I urged her to calm down, but she just grew more agitated. She shouted that all she wanted was for me to look after Pearl for a few days.

"I am not your babysitter!"

"You been taken care of that other girl—Maculata's little sister!"

That stopped me for a moment. What else did she know about me? But now wasn't the time to ask. I pushed her back down in my father's chair and took the baby from her. I was cooing to her and rocking her gently and just about had her settled down when we heard someone scream. Still holding Pearl, I hurried from the room to the top of the stairs, calling, "Ruthy, Tanya, what's going on?"

At the bottom of the stairs, Didimo looked up at me.

Coming up behind me, Kiesha saw him and screamed.

Chapter 38

After that, all I remember are disconnected images. Didimo pointing his gun at us—well, mainly he was pointing it at Kiesha, but I was right there beside her. We ran back into my studio. I kicked the door shut behind me and heard him shouting as he came up the stairs.

Kiesh was shouting, too. "Give her to me! Give her to me!" and trying to pull Pearl from my arms.

We hid ourselves in the bathroom that was between my parents' old bedroom and the other bedroom next to it. I left both doors to the bathroom slightly open so I could see which room he came in. I wanted to be sure I ran the right way. I know it seems incredible that I would think all this out in the midst of my panic, but I did. I had a plan. Not a good one, but a plan anyhow.

When he burst into my parents' bedroom—my studio—I pulled the bathroom door shut and locked it. Then Kiesh and I tried to get through the other bathroom door at the same time, which held us up for a split second. We charged across the other bedroom and out into the hall where we headed back to the head of the stairs, which took us right by the door to my studio.

As we ran down the hall, I pulled over the bed frames and mattresses that I had propped up against the wall when I converted my parents' bedroom into a studio, but I did this without stopping. I pulled things over behind me with my free hand—the one that wasn't pressing Pearl to my chest. I didn't think they would stop him, but I hoped they would slow him down.

Something did. But I doubt if it was the frames and mattresses. Nor do I think it was that feeble bolt on the bathroom door. I think what held him up and gave us time to reach the stairs were the pictures in my studio. I think he must have paused—for a moment at least—when he found himself surrounded by all those nightmarish faces I painted last winter—all of them silently shouting, "Me! Me! Look at me!"

In any case, Kiesh, Pearl, and I got to the stairs and started down before he burst out of the guest bedroom behind us.

Pearls was squirming, so I held her tight with both hands as I raced down the stairs, but since I couldn't swing my arms to keep my balance, I had to go faster and faster to stay upright, which forced me to leap the last two steps. I landed wrong, turned one ankle and nearly fell, but managed to stay upright as I went staggering across the living room. Hitting the far wall with my right shoulder, I caromed sideways, spun once around, and plopped, involuntarily, on the couch.

I was done.

And here he came down the stairs after us.

Kiesh was screaming. Pearl was screaming. So was I, I think.

What I didn't know was that when Didimo charged into the living room, shouting, "Where are you, bitch?" Amanda was still in the house. She was in the kitchen giving Tanya last minute instructions and telling her goodbye.

Grabbing the girls, she raced out the back door into the backyard, around the corner of the house and down the drive-

way to the street where her car was parked. Telling the girls to lock the doors, lie on the floor, and stay put, she unlocked her glove compartment ("Glove compartment"—that's another one of those words, isn't it?) and took out her pistol. I wish I knew what kind it was but I don't.

And then that amazing woman cocked it or whatever one does to guns and started back up the driveway, pausing only to wave the pistol at an astonished Mrs. Harrison, my next door neighbor, who was out watering her zinnias, and tell her to call the police.

I would hesitate to trust Amanda with my investments. (She worked for a broker for a while.) She's too impatient, too daring. Or with my husband, if I had one. Or, maybe I just need to get to know her better. But I know her well enough now to know that if I ever have an appointment at the O.K. Corral and am walking towards it, there is nobody I would rather have fall into step beside me than Amanda Jenson Cameron Butler.

To slightly recast a stanza from another poem I memorized in junior high, back in the days before the wizards of education concluded that memorization would curdle the brains of the young:

> *In the world's broad field of battle,*
> *In the bivouac of life,*
> *She was not like driven cattle!*
> *She was a hero in the strife!*

At the time, however, I still thought she had left the house, so I had no idea that she had already come back in through the kitchen and was now standing behind me in the doorway to the dining room.

I think Spence told me the quarterback used to beat her up. In any case, something bad happened to her before she met Spence, and for years she'd been nursing a grudge against her ex, or the police, or her lawyer, or all of them together, and had been transforming her rage into a determination to "succeed"—meaning to get rich. Maybe if I'd known her story, I would have liked her better all along. Maybe someday she'll tell me what happened to her. Whatever it was, her previous experiences had primed her for this particular afternoon. Didimo bursting into her life like that allowed her to express some long repressed aggression.

When he came bounding down the stairs from the second floor, I was on the couch, hugging Pearl, resigned to my fate. Kiesha was on her knees in front of me, hugging both me and Pearl, and we were all screaming!

Then I heard shots.

Didimo slipped on the stairs, caught himself, sat up and fired through the railing but not at us. I twisted around and saw . . . For a second I didn't know what I saw.

Amanda. She was on her way to a funeral, remember? Black dress. Black shoes. Black hat. I bet she even had on black underwear. She doesn't do things by halves. Then I realized this apparition had a gun and was shooting at Didimo.

And he was shooting back.

Distant sirens.

He heard them, too. He leaped down the remaining stairs and raced right past us to the front door where he paused for one last wild shot. I'd seen this scene before—in the Western movies my father used to take me to. I doubt if Didimo saw many Westerns, but I bet the same basic scene is in a lot of movies—not that I go to many movies, but I've seen previews, and I think Didimo was seeing himself in one of those movies where the star is always making a dramatic escape—like jumping through a window or off a roof. I didn't think this at the time, of course. At the time I was too hysterical to think anything.

Then he was gone, and we were still there. Still alive. Little Pearl was the only one still screaming and her screams had settled into a regular, evenly spaced pattern. The silence in the room as she sucked in another breath was intense.

The sirens had stopped a moment earlier.

Sobbing, Kiesha pried her daughter from my too-tight grip, and began cooing to her.

Amanda stalked past us on her high heels. She was holding her gun with both hands, ready for anything. Was she seeing herself in a movie, too? She was radiant. I've never seen her so beautiful. And this was the woman who referred to "Mr. Turkey" at Christmas and had been known to talk baby-talk to her husband.

She grinned at me. A scary grin.

Outside, a car roared and squealed as it took off.

We all rushed out on the porch. Halfway down the block, a police car was parked sideways, blocking the street. Didimo's car swerved into a driveway, and then he drove across the flat front lawns of the houses across the street, crashing through the Jamison's hedge, plowing through the Gerhard's flower bed.

I was told later what happened next. At the far end of the block, his car erupted from between two curbside trees and shot out into the cross street, just in time for its path to intersect those of two cars coming from opposite directions. Metal banged, scraped, ripped, and wrinkled. Frames twisted. Glass splash-webbed, pebbled, and splattered. Doors caved in and popped open. Didimo's car was bent this way at one end and that way at the other. His gas tank exploded.

The driver of the westbound car stumbled out of his car on his own. Two boys going by on their bikes threw them aside and managed to unbuckle the grandmother who was driving the eastbound car and pull her out before she was incinerated.

There was no hope for Didimo.

All up and down the block, dogs barked and people came out of their houses to tell each other what happened. Cars with flashing lights and floating wails came and went. Hoses were unrolled. Hydrants were turned on. People on gurneys were rolled to ambulances. Uniformed patrolmen stood idly about. Two or three of them walked from tree to tree sealing off half the neighborhood with yellow tape. Firemen shouted. And evil smelling smoke boiled up above the treetops down at the corner.

Chapter 39

The police were still at my house when Maria came by to pick up Ruthy. I introduced her to Mark and to Amanda, but not to Kiesh, who was in the den being interviewed by two women detectives. And while Amanda and Tanya and Ruthy were all talking at the same time, telling Maria what had happened, I took Mark aside and told him Maria was Immaculata's mother.

"Whose mother?"

"The girl, you know. Last Fall, at the 7-Eleven. The girl over there in the yellow dress is her little sister, Ruthy."

"Someone's on your porch," called Amanda.

A woman was out there arguing with the patrolman who was posted beside the door. I opened the door. "Vern!" I exclaimed.

"Fern," he/she corrected me. "What's going on, dear? Look here. I brought you a present."

"I don't believe it," I said, looking at him. There were three smashed cars down at the end of my block. One of them was still burning, making an awful stink. There were I-didn't-know-how-many people dead or injured. Emergency vehicles were coming and going. One of those TV vans was parked in a neighbor's driveway. The street was full of police cars, policemen, and gawkers. My house was full of bullet holes. My body was full of aches, pains, bruises, and scrapes that were just beginning to announce themselves, and here was "Fern," perfectly made-up, coifed, and perfumed. (One of her false eyelashes was slightly crooked, but that could happen to any of us.) She was surreally feminine. And she was offering me a hatbox.

"You look awful, dear. What happened?"

"I don't believe this," I repeated stupidly.

"You can't go in there," said the patrolman.

"Don't believe what?" asked Amanda who had come to see what was keeping me.

"Yes, what don't you believe?" simpered Fern.

"Lady, this is a crime scene. You can't go in."

I called Mark who, without even asking who Fern was, told the officer at the door to let her in. (Did he recognize Vern/Fern? I never asked.) I introduced "her" to Amanda and Maria and the girls. Behind Fern's back Mark grinned at me and raised his eyebrows. I frowned at him. He laughed.

Ruthy, who had hold of his hand, asked him what was so funny.

"Nothing," he said, grinning again. They sat down together on the piano bench.

"Barbara, look what I brought you," said Fern. And with a flourish, he/she removed the top of the hatbox. "Happy birthday. I made it myself."

"I'm hungry," said Tanya."

Suddenly everybody was hungry.

"Do you have any ice-cream, Barbara?" asked Amanda, who had taken off her hat and her shoes.

So in the middle of everything we all had chocolate cake and ice cream. Kiesh and Pearl, and the two detectives who had been with her in the den, came out and joined us. Mark told the patrolman on the porch to come in and have some, too.

The next half hour was special. I didn't realize this at the time, not consciously. But I must have realized it because at some point I started weeping. Not crying or sobbing, just letting tears slide down my face. Partly it was relief, I guess. Mark patted my hand. But it was more than just relief. Partly it was the cake and the ice cream. It was all so unexpected.

It didn't last, of course. As Mark was leaving he said to me, "I guess you painted those pictures in that room upstairs."

He had been through my studio, of course, along with a photographer taking pictures of bullet holes. I said "yes," and he said, "They're pretty good, aren't they?"

Wow, a compliment. Most people don't even notice my pictures. I think they think I bought them somewhere. But I guess Mark notices things because he's a detective.

I said, "You should see the ones in my bedroom."

He looked startled, and I, realizing what I'd said, laughed and explained it was "my bedroom" when I was a little girl, but that now I was using it as a storeroom, while I slept in what used to be my brother's bedroom. I didn't mention that I was using my parents' bedroom as a studio. (Why does everything have to be so complicated?)

Maria and Ruthy wanted to know what we were laughing at, which caused us to laugh some more. Across the room, I saw Fern cross her legs, adjust her hem, and pat her lips with her napkin.

Catching my look, she called over "Now do you believe?"

I wanted to ask him, "Believe what?" but I had to say goodbye to Amanda and when I turned around he—she, I mean—was leaving with Maria and Ruthy.

"I'll call you," he said, giving me a hug.

Chapter 40

That night, I couldn't sleep. The pills Amanda gave me didn't work, and I was afraid to take more of them. My mind kept replaying what had happened. I could feel myself racing into my studio, then into the bathroom, then through the other bedroom, and back out into the hall, and then pell-mell down the stairs with little Pearl in my arms.

I lay very still but my heart beat faster every time I replayed in my imagination my careering, careening, caroming attempt to escape—an attempt that always ended with me plopping on the couch. Finally I got up from my bed and sat sideways on the sill of an open window and looked outside. The moonlight made the familiar back yards look like another world. One of the Hanson's kids had left a bike outside. His or her father wouldn't like that. It was all so normal—and so unreal.

A few hours earlier, people had been shooting guns in my house. It didn't seem possible. I had to keep reminding myself it had really happened.

I've read references to "cleansing violence." I didn't feel cleansed, even though I'd taken two baths. All I felt was nervous, feeble, and helpless. Deep breaths, I kept telling myself. Breathe with your stomach.

Didimo was dead, along with that man at the filling station. . . . What was his name? Bill, yes, old Bill. Also Immaculata, and my parents, and billions of other people since the beginning of time. Me, too, someday, and so what?

Spence keeps telling me I have to make plans—for my life after teaching, he means. But "the best laid plans of mice and men gang oft agley," do they not? And what difference does it make if they do? What difference does anything make? Teaching English, for instance. Where now are the literary lords of yesteryear? Chaucer, Dryden, Pope, Byron, Wordsworth, Tennyson, Longfellow, Eliot, Auden. . . . At one with Shelly's "Ozymandias" is where. Come to think of it, where is "literature"? That's another one of those words, isn't it? Hard to believe that not so very long ago ordinary people read "literature" without ever "taking a course in it"—indeed, without even knowing it was "literature." "Education"? Same thing. What, pray tell, does it mean these days "to have an education"? How can you tell if a person has one?

I had spent years working in an old-fashioned education factory designed to produce mass-men on an assembly line. Fortunately the system was never very efficient, so in spite of all its requirements and programs and examinations, a lot of kids went on to become real people, each one following his or her own unauthorized, zig-zaggy path.

Of course a lot of them might have actually learned something if they hadn't been kept busy "satisfying requirements."

Sitting in the window, watching someone's cat slink across the Hansen's moonlit backyard, I felt like I had been sucked into one of those tar pits where they find all those dinosaur bones. Old Miss Nitpicky, that was me, a doomed dinosaur who was sinking into the tar and struggling to get out.

I had to get out.

So once again, I pulled up my nightgown and sprayed my sore muscles with Kool-n-Fit. Then I sat down at my father's old desk, picked up his fat, old-fashioned fountain pen, and without turning on the light—the moon was very bright—I began to write. I wrote:

"Call me crazy. You won't be the first, but last October…"

Epilogue

Gus says I have to tell how things turned out for everyone. I told her I didn't know anything about that. However, she used to be an assistant district attorney and has retained the tenacity characteristic of those people. So, here's as much as I know.

DIDIMO

Mark told me those tests they do on guns showed Didimo's gun was the one used to kill Immaculata and to wound the clerk at Kim Soo's, but it was not the one used to kill old Bill. I don't think they ever caught the guy who did that.

Apparently, Didimo robbed stores for thrills. A sideline. His real business was providing teenage call girls to clients at expensive hotels. He had two adult partners who enlisted the aid of various hotel employees.

Why did he go berserk? He was high. The autopsy showed that, but he was also on the run. His partners had been arrested, and the police were waiting at his house to pick him up. He knew this and blamed Kiesha for turning him in. He beat her up, also her mother, and trashed their house, but in the middle of all this, he had to go to the bathroom and nature is not to be denied. While he was sitting there with his pants around his ankles, Kiesh grabbed Pearl and took off. She came to me because she thought he would never link the two of us. She was wrong. Didimo wasn't stupid—not at all.

KIESHA

Kiesh and Tia were both on his payroll, but when Kiesh learned she was pregnant, she refused to take any more "assignments." Didimo ordered her to have an abortion. She refused. And after Pearl was born, she refused to resume her "duties." (His word.) He told her she wasn't following the rules—his rules. He was a great rule-maker. After all these years, the whole thing still makes me so sad. He could have been ... Well, I don't know what he could have been but he could have been better. Of course, that's true of all of us. Anyhow, Kiesh moved downstate to live with her grandmother. I wrote her several times, but she never answered.

TIA

Her lawyer hired a ghost to write a book about the life of a teenage call girl. It was on the Best Seller list for over a month. Even after the ghost and the lawyer took their cuts, she made a sizeable sum. She was on several television shows and the cover of *Vanity Fair.* I heard she was working as a model but lost track of her for several years. Then she became briefly famous again when she married the mayor of London. I don't know how this happened or how the marriage worked out. Life is so much stranger than I used to think it was.

VERN/FERN

He quit teaching and went into business with Maria. They opened a bigger beauty salon in a better neighborhood. Sometimes he worked as Fern; sometimes as Vern. He became a local celebrity. Spence found them their space and arranged the lease. Amanda helped them create a business plan and found them a banker.

MARK

He married the waitress he was flirting with at that place where we had lunch. I like her. She's very funny. They have two sons, Matthew and Mark Junior. When he retired from the police force, he and his wife opened a restaurant.

RUTHY

She began working in the office of her mother's new salon even before she graduated from high school. Responsibility agreed with her. She went to college and majored in business.

SWEET

He didn't know anything about anything. But he was an embarrassment to The Powers That Be. They couldn't just fire him. The assistant principals have a union, too. So they sent him off on a sabbatical, and that was the last I heard of him.

SPENCE AND AMANDA

He sold his real estate company when Amanda retired from C. T. Denbow, and they moved to Florida.

TANYA

Just like her mother, she married her high school sweetheart. Amanda raged and despaired. But Tanya's high school romance worked out better than her mother's. When Tanya told Roy (her husband) that she was pregnant, he dropped out of college and went to work as an apprentice plumber. His uncle owned a plumbing business. Over the next few years, Tanya taught herself court reporting. Now they both have their own businesses—also four children, three dogs, and a parrot.

SCOTT

He was accepted at several colleges, but at the last minute he joined the army. His father was stunned. "Why?" he kept asking. When Scott's enlistment was up, he went to college for a year but didn't like it. He played in a band for a while. Then he did voice-overs and seems to have made a pretty good living doing that—something his father still cannot understand. At present he is the editor of an online magazine about the New York theatre.

EDDY

When Scott was in the army, he sent me a postcard. I saved it. I'm looking at it right now. It says: "Met a Marine officer who says he had you at Pershing. Big guy. Basketball type. Says to tell you Eddy says Hi."

By that time, I'd changed a lot, too.

DESMOND BIRDWHISTLE

The villain. The rich, immoral capitalist who took advantage of a mere child, a student, an intern. What twaddle. Tia knew what she was doing. It was Desmond who was full of illusions. Oh, sure, he responded to her "charms." But he also thought he was educating her. Helping her. He'd seen too many movies. I have always thought of myself as a fairly innocent person, but compared to Desmond, I am a woman of the world.

He took Tia to museums and concerts. He gave her books. Our very own Professor Higgins, swollen with despotic dreams of molding and shaping. I can appreciate how he felt. It's the teaching sickness.

Desmond's legal problem had to do with whether or not he and Tia began their affair before or after her eighteenth birthday. Tia didn't realize why this was significant at first. But when she did, she insisted their affair began after her birthday. This infuriated everyone—her court-appointed lawyer, the district attorney, the reporters covering the case, her mother. They all wanted to see the mighty Desmond brought down. But Tia, bless her, refused to "cooperate." The D.A. threatened to send her to jail for something. (They can always find "something" these days.) But all the publicity had brought her to the attention of a big-time lawyer. He took over her case for a percentage of whatever she would make from the book he would have someone write for her.

Anyhow, though Lavinia divorced Des and he had to resign from Denbow, he was never charged with anything.

All this took months, but after it was over, Amanda invited Des to dinner—and me, too, because she said he said he wanted to meet me. She said he'd seen one of my paintings—the one in her office—and had liked it.

At that dinner he said he was writing a book.

"What about?" I asked, certain it would be about the scandal—his side of the story.

"Horace," he said.

"Horace who?" I blurted.

He said, "The Roman poet."

I was so embarrassed. I thought men like him just smoked cigars, played golf, and made deals. It had never occurred to me that he might *translate Latin!* He explained that he'd majored in classics as an undergraduate. His ex-wife—Lavinia—

was his Latin teacher's daughter. He said he was very disturbed about the quality of the published translations of Horace.

I could hardly keep my face straight. Who gave a hoot about Horace anymore?

Well, he did. And I cracked up. I laughed until I cried. He wanted to know what was funny. I told him he wasn't what I'd expected. He said, well, I wasn't what he expected, either, and there we were—off and running.

He asked if I had more paintings, and a week later, he came to my house. He liked my cartoons. I gave him a couple. He offered money. I refused to take it. My cartoons are just doodles. A week or so later, he asked me to illustrate his book on Horace and insisted on paying me.

I don't understand the points he makes in that book. But as an ex-English teacher I appreciate the epigraph he chose. It's from one of his own translations.

> *An antique word is mysteriously revived.*
> *A buzzword goes mysteriously extinct.*
> *The whims of the goddess, Usage, shape our speech*
> *and, thus, shape half, at least, of what we think.*

He published his book himself and sold sixteen copies of it—two to classmates from college, two to academics, and the rest to befuddled relatives or business associates. His second book was about Ausonius—"the best Latin poet of the fourth century." Wow! Well, I didn't paint for money and he didn't write for money, so we were even.

Yes, reader, I married him.

> *Life will never go*
> *according to the epistles.*
> *Expecting whistles, flutes;*
> *Expecting flutes, its whistles.*

Do you know that poem? It's Spanish: *"cuando pitos, flautas, / cuando flautas, pitos."* And, yes, I speak Spanish. This isn't the story of my life, you know. There's a lot about me I haven't told you.